"I hope you like it…even if it is just for a little while."

He opened the box.

"Oh, my God, Bradley. Is that real?"

His face screwed into a wry smile. "Oh, yes. The women you'll be meeting tonight are intimately familiar with jewelry. They'd spot a fake in an instant."

"That's the most gorgeous diamond I've ever seen."

He smiled. "I thought so, too."

Amber was aware that they had come to an awkward moment. Did she take it out of the box and slip it on her finger? Did he? Outside of her fantasies, this was the only time she'd ever been offered an engagement ring. She wished this proposal wasn't make-believe. Everything was perfect—the man, the moment, the stunning jewel.…

Dear Reader,

What happens when six brides and six grooms wed for *convenient* reasons? Well... In Donna Clayton's *Daddy Down the Aisle*, a confirmed bachelor becomes a FABULOUS FATHER—with the love of an adorable toddler...and his beautiful bride.

One night of passion leaves a (usually) prim woman expecting a BUNDLE OF JOY! In Sandra Steffen's *For Better, For Baby*, the mom-to-be marries the dad-to-be—and now they have nine months to fall in love....

From secretarial pool to wife of the handsome boss! Well, for a while. In Alaina Hawthorne's *Make-Believe Bride*, she hopes to be his Mrs. Forever—after all, that's how long she's loved him!

What's a rancher to do when his ex-wife turns up on his doorstep with amnesia and a big, juicy kiss? In Val Whisenand's *Temporary Husband*, he simply "forgets" to remind her that they're divorced....

Disguised as lovey-dovey newlyweds on a honeymoon at the Triple Fork Ranch, not-so-loving police partners uncover their own wedded bliss in Laura Anthony's *Undercover Honeymoon*....

In debut author Cathy Forsythe's *The Marriage Contract*, a sexy cowboy proposes a marriage of convenience, but when his bride discovers the real reason he said "I do"—watch out!

I hope you enjoy all six of our wonderful CONVENIENTLY WED titles this month—and all of the Silhouette Romance novels to come!

Regards,

Melissa Senate
Senior Editor

Please address questions and book requests to:
Silhouette Reader Service
U.S.: 3010 Walden Ave., P.O. Box 1325, Buffalo, NY 14269
Canadian: P.O. Box 609, Fort Erie, Ont. L2A 5X3

MAKE-BELIEVE BRIDE

Alaina Hawthorne

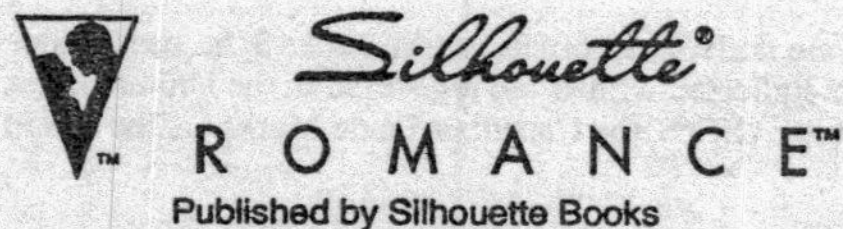

Published by Silhouette Books
America's Publisher of Contemporary Romance

Thanks as always to Marilyn Amann, Pat Kay, Carla Luan and Heather MacAllister who make all things possible.

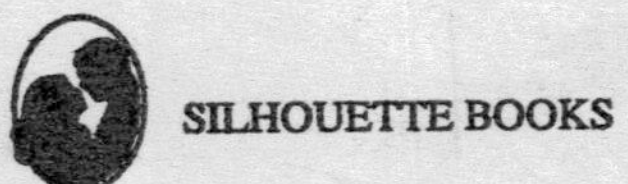

ISBN 0-373-19164-2

MAKE-BELIEVE BRIDE

This edition published by arrangement with Harlequin Books S.A.

Printed in U.S.A.

Books by Alaina Hawthorne

Silhouette Romance

Out of the Blue #672
The Bridal Path #1029
My Dearly Beloved #1069
Make-Believe Bride #1164

ALAINA HAWTHORNE,

a native Texan, has been writing fiction and nonfiction since she was a teenager. Her first Silhouette Romance novel won the Romance Writers of America's RITA Award for Best First Book. She lives in Houston with Sallie, her rottweiler, and loves hearing from her readers. Write to Alaina at P.O. Box 820342 Houston TX 77282.

Engagement Announcement

Estelle "Grandy" Dunwoody-Ackerman
is pleased to announce
the engagement of her grandson,

Bradley Alan Ackerman
to
Amber Louise Oakland

The handsome groom-to-be is the V.P. of Ackerman Drilling, and according to his grandmother, way past the age when he should have married!

The bride-to-be is also an Ackerman employee and is working toward her education degree. Sources say the couple met in the elevator.

Although no wedding date has been set as of yet, a fete in the couple's honor has been planned at Columbine Hall by "Grandy" Ackerman herself.

Chapter One

"What on earth...?" Amber Oakland muttered to herself as she pulled into the underground parking lot of the Ackerman Drilling Company. She had assumed that she'd have her pick of parking places every day, including executive slots by the entrance. After all, her shift didn't start until five-thirty, and by that time nearly all the daytime employees' cars were long gone. Today, however, there seemed to be cars in every available space. She turned down the radio, finding the music suddenly distracting.

Just outside the glass doors of the underground entrance she saw two young men in ill-fitting and presumably rented tuxedos pacing nervously. As she drove past, the cork board leaning against the wall and bristling with car keys identified them as contracted valet-parking attendants.

"What *is* this?" she said as she began to weave her way up and down the aisles, each pass taking her farther from the entrance. Finally, in the most distant corner of the lot, she found a place and nosed her Toyota pickup between a sleek, four-door Mercedes and a Lincoln the size of a gravel barge.

Amber had never seen so many luxury cars in the Ackerman parking garage and couldn't imagine what was going on. She vaguely remembered seeing a notice posted about a reception for the ambassador to somewhere or other, but she'd paid little attention to it at the time. After all, she'd been working at Ackerman only one month, and she knew the possibility of anyone on the night staff being included in any sort of executive function fell somewhere between remote and nonexistent.

Not that she would have been offended. In fact, anonymity was one of the reasons her new job suited her perfectly. She had little involvement with the people she worked for, and therefore her job, though demanding in its own way, held little to distract her from her studies.

The schedule suited her perfectly, too—seven days on, seven days off. The most important thing about the job, however, was that her shift started late in the afternoon, so she had all day to go to school. Finally, after three years of managing only one or two classes a semester, she was making real progress toward her degree.

Whenever the grueling schedule got her down, whenever she was treated with contempt or impatience by the staff because she was new and inexperienced, whenever the crazy hours seemed to separate her from everyone in the "normal world," she just reminded herself of the reason she was doing this. Only two more years and she'd graduate. That thought alone was enough to make her swallow her pride, drown her exhaustion with buckets of coffee and get on with the job.

She killed the truck's engine, gathered up her books and opened her door. Immediately a suffocating tide of humid July air rolled in and obliterated the remnants of air-conditioning. All day the Houston sun had beaten down on the building, heating the still, underground air like a pressure cooker. Amber knew that the walk all the way back to the entrance would be long and wilting. She slid out of the truck and headed toward the doors. She had nearly reached the entrance when she heard the shriek of tires on asphalt.

In moments a black, mud-splattered, four-wheel drive careened into view and came to a rocking halt at the valet station. At almost the exact instant the vehicle stopped, the driver's side door exploded open, and a man in a black dinner jacket jumped out and ran around the front of the vehicle. Although he never looked at Amber, she had a perfect view of his face. The minute she saw him, her world tilted and shifted into slow motion.

She instantly absorbed everything about him: the strong, square jaw and heavy swing of thick, sun-streaked hair; the way he moved with an athlete's competence and economy; broad shoulders that angled down to narrow hips and long legs. His unbuttoned coat flapped away from a blinding white shirt to reveal his flat stomach.

But it was something other than his physical appearance that stopped her. He had an aura of vitality—an almost animal magnetism—that reached her even at a distance. The urgency of his movements and the expression around his eyes communicated consternation, but just as he rounded the front of the Jeep, Amber saw that one corner of his mouth was lifted, and his tanned cheek dimpled slightly.

Her soul leaped. *It's you.*

Unexpected tears stung her eyes, and her throat closed.

He skidded to a stop at the passenger door, yanked it open and offered his hand. Amber couldn't see his companion behind the dark glass.

Look this way. See me.

A flash of sapphire-colored silk appeared, incongruous beside the spray of red mud on the door. Amber heard the hiss of breath exhaled in disgust. Then a woman stepped away from the door and snatched her hand out of his. "A truck," she accused, her consonants cracking like a ruler on knuckles. "I can't believe you'd bring me here in this . . . this *thing*."

"I'm sorry, Tovah. I'll kill Rudy tomorrow, but the damned car wasn't ready, and I was already late."

His baritone, brisk but conciliatory, curled through Amber, condensed into a warm coil in her middle and ignited dormant nerve endings.

"You could have ordered a limo. Even a cab..."

Amber didn't hear the rest of the tirade because his words were finally sinking in. *I'm sorry, Tovah.* The woman had to be Tovah Stein. From sightings on the society page, Amber thought she recognized the striking face and all five feet, eleven inches of rail-thin, old-money, high-fashion bone structure. Amber swallowed and tried to recover some composure. Less than twenty feet away from her, Tovah Stein was hissing like a furious goose and rattling a ransom in diamonds at *him*.

Amber's soul mate. Her beloved.

Wait a minute. This is insane! You've never even seen him before.

But there was no denying it. Every fiber, every cell and atom in her body strained toward him. Knew him. Even if she were struck blind at that moment, she knew she would recognize that face by touch. She would know it better than her own.

Stop this now. This is stupid.

But something inside Amber—an emotional imperative that had little respect for good sense or even good manners—made a decision for her. She moved forward, closing the distance between them.

He would see her just as she had seen him. Then he, too, would have the same flash of recognition. She would fling down her books, and he would drop that ridiculous woman's elbow and sweep Amber up into his arms, and away to his...construction site? Veterinary practice? Charter airline?

She didn't care. At that moment all that mattered was getting his attention.

So far he hadn't even looked her way. Instead he snatched the claim ticket from the valet like a relay runner taking a handoff, jammed it into his pocket and herded his icy-eyed date toward the glass doors.

Amber practically lunged after them. If she hurried they would arrive at the door at the same time. Maybe they would collide in the doorway. At the very least she could ride up the elevator with him.

Thoughts flitted through her mind. *I'm wearing blue jeans, running shoes and a Houston Rockets T-shirt. My hair is in a ponytail, and I'm not wearing any makeup.*

All of that was unimportant. She had cell-deep knowledge. Never, in all of her twenty-seven years, had she felt anything like this. This had to be destiny. She recognized it from descriptions she'd read in books.

Omigod, what if they're married?

She felt a twist of fear, followed by an almost sickening relief. Of course they weren't married. Tovah Stein hadn't married anyone lately. Amber was positive she would have read about it.

The couple was now only a few feet in front of her. He pulled the door open and stepped aside. Tovah swept imperiously past him just as Amber managed to insinuate herself in his peripheral vision. He stood away for her to precede him but didn't even glance at her.

Tall, Amber thought, as she slid past his shoulder, taller even than Tovah—at least six-one or two. Even in shoes Amber was five-seven on her tallest days, five-nine if she wore suicide heels. With rising desperation she realized their moment was passing and she was going to have to say something to him or he'd miss it altogether.

"Thanks," she said brightly.

"Mmm," he replied. His eyes were trained down the hallway where Tovah's heels were clicking angrily on the travertine.

As soon as Amber was safely through the door, he shot by her, his long legs moving him toward the elevator doors that would take him forever out of her life. She broke into a power walk and arrived at the doors just in time to stop them from closing.

Tovah gave her a withering look and raised one penciled eyebrow so high it almost disappeared under the blue-black fringe of her gamine-cut bangs. Amber felt a stab of envy. Just like Spock, she thought. I wish I could do that. How did she learn how to do it? she wondered. Probably hours and hours of practice in front of a mirror. Amber had never spent hours and hours in front of a mirror doing anything.

The doors closed with a muted thump, and Amber saw that the button for the sixth floor had been punched. The night staff, wedged between Supply and Telecommunications, occupied a windowless cubicle on the first floor. She toyed momentarily with the idea of riding all the way up with them, pushing Tovah out and then pulling the Emergency Stop. Probably too obvious, she thought.

With an efficient hydraulic hum, the elevator began its ascent. You'd better punch your floor, she thought. No, maybe not. Riding all the way up with them would give her more time to get his attention. He still hadn't noticed her, but was now deeply engaged in buttoning his jacket and tugging his cuffs down. Amber had five floors to make an impression and was trying to decide just how to do it when Tovah spoke.

"I hope you know I'm not riding home in that thing, Bradley," she said in a glacial voice.

Bradley. What a perfect name. So masculine, yet sensitive. Mr. and Mrs. Bradley... What? Bradley and Amber Something-or-other. Seconds and floors and the chance of a lifetime flew past.

One part of her was saying, *You've lost your mind,* while the other part yelled, *Say something! Do something unforgettable before he's gone and you never see him again.*

"I understand," he said. "I'll call a Towne Car—"

"Thanks," she snapped, "but I'm sure *someone* will be here to drive me."

The elevator stopped, and the doors opened to a swell of party sounds—clinking glassware, polite murmurings and muted music. Tovah lifted her chin and stepped forward, Bradley followed, raking a tanned, long-fingered hand through his hair. He was going, going...

"Enjoy the party," Amber blurted.

She was distantly aware that Tovah was giving her a look that would vaporize stainless steel. So what. Bradley, however, turned, blinked slightly, and her eyes finally joined his—emerald green and roiling with determination, humor and introspection all at once. Their gaze held, and for just an instant he hesitated, and then that same corner of his mouth lifted.

"Thanks," he said.

The doors closed and silence settled around her. She felt drained and shaky—just like the time she'd barely moved her car off the tracks before the express roared by. At least he saw me, she thought. When the doors closed he was still looking at me, I'm sure of that.

She suddenly remembered to breathe. "Oh, for heaven's sake," she muttered. "Of course he was staring at you. 'Enjoy the party.' Good grief, how lame can you get?" She sighed. He would remember her as the poorly dressed stalker who once accosted him in an elevator. If he remembered her at all.

She punched the button for the first floor, and the elevator obediently descended. Shake it off, she told herself. You'll never see him again. You were mistaken about him, anyway. That whole silly episode was just something hormonal. Or atmospheric. Probably PMS or something weird brought on by the full moon or a disastrous planetary alignment.

Liar.

Walking down the hall, she clutched her books to her chest, taking comfort from the feel of them, solid and square, against her thumping heart. When she turned down the hallway, her sneakers squeaked on the polished floor. See, she told herself, this is your real life. You have a job and a goal. You probably just need to get out more. "All work and no play" is making you dull. And neurotic.

But her heart wouldn't stop pounding, and she had the unmistakable feeling that something profound had transpired. But what was it? And what could she hope to do about it?

If you let this slip away, it'll haunt you for the rest of your life.

She took a steadying breath and tried to think logically. I suppose I could go down into the parking lot, get the license number off that truck and have it traced, she thought.

Oh, right, then what? Flowers? Anonymous love poems? He'd call the police, and I wouldn't blame him.

When she walked into the night staff room, Zita Bloom looked up. "Amber! Hi. How was school today?"

"Good," she replied, forcing the corners of her mouth up into a simulated smile.

Zita's eyes clouded. "Are you okay?"

"Yeah, fine."

Zita's eyes narrowed. "Are you sure?"

"Of course. Why do you ask?"

"I guess I'm used to you coming in here all bouncy and enthusiastic. Today you look like you just fell off your bike."

Does it show that much? "Oh, I don't know. I'm just a little rattled I guess. I've never seen so many cars down there before. I had to walk a mile and it's so hot—"

"Did you find a place to park?"

"Just barely."

Tam Underwood walked in from Telecopy. "It's that reception thing."

Amber set her books down. "What's going on?" she asked as casually as she could.

Zita leaned toward the bulletin board and squinted slightly. She was a beautiful woman in her middle forties, curvy, tanned and blond and much too vain to wear her glasses unless it was absolutely necessary. "Let's see, it says 'On Monday the fifth there will be a reception in the sixth floor atrium for Manuel de la Fuentes y Perez, Special Interior Minister of…' someplace I can't pronounce. 'Please do not set trash cans in the hallway as Housekeeping will…' blah, blah, blah."

Tam's eyes danced and she rubbed her palms together. "Goodies tonight."

Zita smiled greedily. "Any idea who catered?"

"No, but it's bound to be primo. You know they'll want to impress this guy. Lease all his country's gas wells and sell them a truckload of down hole pipe."

Amber looked from Tam to Zita. "What are you talking about?"

Zita swiveled in her chair. "Anytime they have a function upstairs, they always have it catered, and after it's all over, we can help ourselves to whatever is left."

"If it's just a late meeting they usually order Chinese or Mexican," Tam said. "But for something like this there's no telling what they'll have. Maybe Italian. Could even be prime rib."

"And nobody minds if we go help ourselves?" Amber asked. "We can just—"

"No, of course not," Zita replied. "The caterers wrap the leftover food and leave it. If we don't take it, the cleaning service just throws it out when they get here."

"What time do they come?"

Zita shrugged. "About six in the morning. They're supposed to have everything cleaned by the time the office opens officially at eight-thirty."

"Once I got a whole honey ham," Tam said. "Hadn't even been touched."

Amber slid into the chair by Zita's desk. "I just rode up the elevator with some people going to the party. I think one of them was Tovah Stein."

Tam nodded. "Ah, yes. The once and future squeeze."

Amber swallowed and studiously picked at one of her short, unpolished nails. "The guy she was with was really... really—"

"Gorgeous?" Zita offered.

"Our resident heartache," Tam added.

Amber looked up. "What do you mean 'resident heartache'? Who is he?"

A sly look crossed Zita's face. "Ah, I think I detect another victim. That, my dear, was Bradley Alan Ackerman, our youngest vice president."

Amber swallowed. She'd heard the name and seen it on company letterhead. *This is where he works! He's been somewhere overhead the whole time I've been here.* She felt her heart pounding again. *This has to be destiny. I'm going to see him again. Probably soon.*

Amber was lost in her own thoughts and suddenly realized she had missed some of what Zita was telling her.

"...and is the grandson of Pope Ackerman who, as you know, founded this company with Estelle Dunwoody-Ackerman."

Amber recognized that name, too. "She's the chairman of the board."

"Exactly," Zita said. "Bradley might be the one to take over the company when his grandmother steps down. *If* she steps down, I mean. The two sisters aren't involved in the business at all, and his uncles are pretty far out of the picture, at least as far as the drilling company."

"But there's the father," Tam said. She wrinkled her nose. "Evil Prince Phillip."

"Why 'evil'?"

"Wait'll you meet him," Zita said. "He's a sarcastic, condescending ass."

"Thinks he's better than everybody," Tam said. "Rude, nasty." She raised her eyebrows. "He's really mean to his wife, Bradley's mother, in front of everybody. I hear he runs around on her like crazy, and she's so sweet—"

"Kind of drippy though," Zita said. "A real Southern belle type, you know. All that moonlight-and-magnolia 'Honey-lamb' and 'Ah do declare' stuff."

"How do you know them so well?" Amber asked. Although she hated gossip, she desperately wanted to bring the conversation back around to the man she intended to... to what? Marry? Seduce? Kidnap?

"I've worked here for fifteen years," Zita said.

"Besides, it's a small company," Tam added. "You just hear things."

"Is he—Bradley, I mean—is he—" she swallowed "—engaged to Tovah?"

Tam snorted. "She wishes."

"They've known each other for a long time, and he's dated her off and on over the years," Zita replied, her hazel eyes wise and amused. "But I don't think our Bradley's ready to settle down."

The phone rang, and Zita glanced down. "Your line, Tam."

"Oh, hell," she muttered, and ducked back into Telecopy.

Amber cleared her throat. "Um, how old is he?"

With a knowing and indulgent smile, Zita reeled off the statistics. "Thirty. No, thirty-one. Never married, no children. He's here every day from six in the morning until about four in the afternoon because he likes to avoid the traffic."

No wonder I haven't seen him before. He's gone by the time I get here.

"He has an apartment in the Riverwood high rise and he spends as much time as he can at the family ranch up in the hill country. The parents have an estate in River Oaks, but Bradley doesn't go there much because he and his father don't get along. Is there anything else you want to know?"

Amber felt herself blushing. Zita obviously recognized a crush when she saw one. "I just saw him and I felt—I mean I really feel that—"

"If it were anyone else I'd say go for it," Zita said quietly, "but I'd hate to see you get hurt."

"Is he a real ladies' man or something?"

"No, nothing like that. Just the opposite, in fact. He's really a great guy, and everyone here likes him, but he's just not the type to settle with one woman. He's dated a lot of gorgeous girls over the years, but never any one girl for very long. Tovah's hung in there because their families are close—you know, oil business, society friends, that kind of thing. Besides, you're smart enough to know that a workplace romance spells disaster—especially if it involves the boss."

"I know," Amber said. "But when I saw him, it was like—I don't know. Something happened. I've never felt anything like it before."

The older woman reached out and patted Amber's hand. "Love at first sight?"

Amber looked up sheepishly. "I'm not really sure. Maybe."

"So, what are you going to do?"

Amber looked at her friend. She had liked Zita the moment they met. She always spoke her mind honestly and wasn't afraid to tell anyone what she thought. She also exuded a quality of nonjudgmental acceptance that made her a natural confidante.

"I don't know. Probably nothing. I can't do anything to jeopardize this job." Amber sighed. "I know it sounds nuts, but nothing like this has ever happened to me before. I think he felt it, too. Do you think there's such a thing as destiny or anything like that?"

Zita smiled. "I hope so."

Amber stood. "Oh, maybe I'm losing my mind. I'd better get to work. What've we got for tonight?"

Zita gave her three full tapes to transcribe and a ninety-page pipeline lease interlineated with scores of tedious revisions—just the type of work Amber knew would keep her mind from wandering. She walked back to her station and flipped on her computer.

Although the machines were top-of-the-line with huge processors and inexhaustible memories, the workstations in the word processing center were really nothing more than cubicles separated by acoustic panels. The panels themselves were gray metal frames upholstered in fabric that appeared to be made of woven dog hair, and the chairs were a complementary color. After one or two eleven-hour days of word processing, Amber decided that the workstations had been comfort-designed by participants of the Spanish Inquisition. With a sigh, she sat down and immersed herself in the Blockhouse Ranch Lease Number One.

At eight-thirty, when the last crisp, white, spell-checked page fell into the output tray, she stood, rolled her shoulders and knuckled the spot at her nape that always ached when she sat too long in one position. A note attached to the marked-up draft had left specific instructions that the revised lease was to be left in the chair of Spencer Bailey, Ackerman's General Counsel and a senior member of the board.

Amber walked back to Zita's desk. "I'm supposed to put this on Mr. Bailey's chair. Do I need a key to get in his office?"

"Nah, everything'll be open late because of the party." Zita glanced at the clock. "I'll get a cart from the mail room, and we can go check out the goodies and see what's left."

Amber had been given a quick, thumbnail tour of the building when she interviewed for the job, but the executive offices weren't included. So far, her trip up the elevator with Bradley and Tovah that afternoon was the only time she'd been to the top floor. Riding up in the elevator again with Zita gave her an uncharacteristically melancholy moment of déjà vu. *What if I never see him again?* she thought, and felt her bottom lip quiver the slightest bit. When the doors slid open, she fell behind and let Zita lead the way.

When Amber had first seen the Ackerman building, she'd thought it looked like a white, stucco bunker—stingy with windows, too, and hopelessly dowdy compared to the metal and glass architectural excesses surrounding it. Although six stories tall, it still managed to look squat and unattractive from the outside. Only the massive oaks and trailing willows with their clusters of scarlet azaleas gave the exterior any charm at all.

The interior of the lower floors wasn't anything to write home about, either. The drywall construction had originally been painted eggshell, but was now scuffed and chair marked. The furniture was all standard company issue: metal desks of battleship gray with matching bookcases and file cabinets. The carpet was low-static, mud-colored, and to call it serviceable would be extravagantly complimentary. And overhead, because keeping up with galloping technology vastly outranked any aesthetic considerations, miles of computer wire trailed like jungle creepers where the ceiling tiles had been removed.

The upper floors, however, were a different story altogether. The walls were sheathed in cool, pink granite, and recessed lighting skillfully illuminated a fortune in watercolors, sculpture and Egyptian statuary. Pope and Estelle Ackerman had made a staggering amount of money wildcatting in the Texas oil fields in the thirties and forties. They both loved travel and archeology, lavishly indulged these passions and unabashedly displayed their treasures.

Each of the executive offices had its own museum-quality paintings or objets d'art and faced the central atrium, which was filled with soaring tropical plants and bromeliads. Jewel-toned Persian rugs lay in gold and scarlet pools on the floor—gifts from Pope's Saudi friends and customers.

Spencer Bailey's office was in the southwest and quietest corner of the top floor. When the building first went up almost thirty years ago, his view had probably been pleasant—if not exactly dramatic—facing, as it then had, endless acres of waving grass and cow pastures. During the seventies and eighties, though, Houston had exploded in all directions, and the Ackerman building which had once been an outpost now sat smack dab in the Westheimer strip-center shopping district.

Bailey's office was neat and looked exactly like Amber imagined a gentleman lawyer's would—a massive mahogany desk centered on a tasteful rug and surrounded by oxblood, buttoned-and-pleated leather furniture. As the note instructed, she left the original draft and revisions in his chair. Just as she turned to leave, her eyes fell on an unexpected treasure.

A collection of photographs in silver frames sat on the credenza behind the enormous leather swivel chair, and the first one she saw revealed a teenage Bradley Ackerman sitting in the cockpit of a small plane. The face was much younger and smoother, but the eyes were the same.

She trailed her fingers over the top of the frame, and studied the office more carefully. Spencer Bailey was obviously more than a business associate—he was a close and longtime family friend. Amber explored his office.

Other photographs hung on the wall behind the desk. She recognized several of Bradley's grandmother from a seated portrait she'd seen behind the reception desk. There were others that hinted at a long and fascinating life: a hunting party in India looking seasick in a swaying howdah; the pyramids at Giza as a backdrop for a beautiful girl on a shaggy, loose-lipped camel; a young woman posed coquettishly in the intake of a jet engine.

There were many more: ribbon cuttings, weddings and gushers spewing ebony rooster tails of crude oil into a grainy black-and-white sky.

"What are you doing?" Zita called from the door.

Amber gave her a sheepish look. "Snooping."

"Well, this is a great place for it, but why don't we get the eats downstairs, and then we can come back. I know where all the neat stuff is. You won't believe what all they've got squirreled away up here."

With a regretful, backward glance, Amber followed her. The reception had been held around the atrium, and the detritus of eighty or so guests littered the low tables, sills and every available horizontal surface. Party napkins, an occasional ashtray, half-empty glasses with pale, diluted contents and unfinished plates of food were all that was left of the murmuring crowd Amber had glimpsed earlier.

She briefly wondered what it would be like to attend ambassadorial receptions and society galas. And what exactly was a gala and how did it differ from other parties? And was the plural *galas* or was it *gali?* For a moment she regretted switching her major. Had she stuck it out in the English Department this was just the kind of thing she'd know.

Zita pushed the cart briskly along, and Amber trailed behind her, stealing quick glances at the artwork. She'd only spent one unsatisfactory semester as an art history major, but she knew she was trotting past a fortune in oil paintings and sculpture. Then another thought occurred to her.

"Um, Zita?"

"Yes."

"Is Bradley Ackerman's office on this floor?"

Zita flung a knowing glance over her shoulder. "Yeees."

Amber let the unasked question hang in the air.

"Let's get the leftovers downstairs, and I'll show you."

Zita led Amber into the conference room, where the caterers had set up the food. Although the party had ended more than an hour earlier, tantalizing smells still hung in the air. The remnants of a rare roast beef were wrapped and waiting on a carving board along with containers filled with stuffed mushrooms, new potatoes in dill sauce and delicate little game hens. On the cold table Amber found artfully arranged fresh fruit and crisp vegetables, salmon sliced paper thin with capers and a blazing hot horseradish.

"How are we going to divide this stuff and get it downstairs?"

"There's a galley kitchen behind that wall," Zita answered. "There should be plenty of plastic bags and aluminum foil. And it's okay to use the plastic bowls and stuff as long as we bring them back tomorrow."

Zita, who'd obviously scavenged parties before, moved efficiently from table to table, sorting and separating what was worth taking. "Oh, look," she called from a little side table. "There must be a dozen loaves of French bread here." She stood with her hands on her hips, then turned to face Amber. "Well I'm sure not leaving this."

At that moment Amber heard the unmistakable chirp of a pager. "That's me," Zita said, picked up the phone on the low table and punched in a phone number. Amber turned and scanned the room, trying to decide where to begin.

"That was Tam." Zita said irritably. "She can't unjam the fax machine. I'll be right back. Why don't you get started? The kitchen's behind that panel."

Amber gathered up two platters of raw vegetables that appeared to have been untouched and took them into the galley. She was dropping them in plastic bags when she heard voices just outside the door.

"...don't know why you're being so stubborn and inconsiderate, Bradley. And after all I've been through. Is it so much to ask?"

A muttered baritone reply slid though the open door and curled into Amber's middle. Nerve endings once again sprang to life.

Bradley? *Her* Bradley?

"Well, it's not exactly like you're asking me to baby-sit another dog for you, is it? You're talking about marriage. A lifetime commitment. Maybe children."

Amber froze. It couldn't be. The party was long over, the guests long gone. She whirled and faced the door, a handful of cauliflower in her right hand, carrots in her left.

Chapter Two

Amber swallowed. "Hi."

Bradley Ackerman tilted his head slightly to the side. "Hello."

Say something. This is your chance.

"I was just..." She lifted both hands to illustrate and cleared her throat. "Vegetables."

His gaze dropped momentarily to her doubled fists, and a smile played around the corners of his mouth. "Oh, yeah," he said. "I thought I recognized them."

Amber smiled and laughed a little. "Zita and I were, em—"

"I know. If I'm working late I do it, too." His eyes dropped to her jeans and sneakers and returned to her face. "So, you work here?"

"Night staff. I'm Amber Ackerm—Oakland. Amber Oakland," she said, feeling the rise of a furious blush. "I'm in night word processing."

"Nice to meet you," he said. "Bradley Ackerman." He started to lift his arm to offer her a handshake, then grinned and let it fall. "You must be new."

She nodded. "I've been here about a month."

They had been standing in opposite corners of the tiny kitchen, and the spell of stillness suddenly broke. Bradley moved to the refrigerator, opened it and grabbed a couple of canned sodas. "I hope you like working here," he said without looking at her. He backed out, saluting her with a frosty red can. "I'm sure I'll see you around."

He was gone. Amber stood motionless for the space of three heartbeats, then covered her face with the fistfuls of cold vegetables and folded herself into a cringe of embarrassment. "Stupid," she said. "Stupid, stupid, stupid."

Another chance down the tubes, she thought. You started to introduce yourself as Amber *Ackerman.* He had to have heard that. He'll think you're a kook. She looked down at herself, her T-shirt, faded jeans and sneakers. Yes, she thought, a very poorly dressed kook.

The casual dress code for the night staff had been another thing that had appealed to her so much. Since they didn't show up until everyone else was gone, as long as their clothes were clean and decent, nobody minded if the staff dressed down. Way down. Amber had never given her clothes another thought until now.

"I do have nice dresses," she said aloud. "Plenty of them. Somewhere."

She would have berated herself further, but suddenly, coming through the wall she heard two voices. One female, the other unmistakable. Nerve endings strained toward the sound like magnetized needles homing toward the pole.

"Even if we do get the contract," the female voice said, "it doesn't mean we're out of the woods. It's not like the old days, you know."

"I know, Grandy," he said. "There's a lot more competition for every dollar."

Grandy. He must be talking to his grandmother. The office on the other side of the wall obviously belonged to the Ackerman chairman of the board. Amber frowned slightly.

Estelle Dunwoody-Ackerman must be past seventy. The voice Amber heard was certainly mature, but by no means old or quavering. She recognized the tone of a woman who was used to getting her way, a voice imbued with vitality and the snap of command.

"And that's exactly why you should do this for me," Grandy said, and then her voice did take on a kind of tiredness. "After all, I'm not getting any younger."

There was a pause, and for a moment Amber couldn't hear anything. She wondered if they'd moved to the far corner of the room and felt tempted to press her ear against the wall.

This is deliberately eavesdropping on someone else's private conversation, she thought reproachfully. She'd never done anything like that before. Well, nothing she could remember at that very moment. She teetered in a moment of moral indecision, then leaned her tired head and shoulders against the wood paneling. This is not eavesdropping, she rationalized—it's resting.

A sudden bark of laughter came through the wall, and she jumped away flinging cauliflower over her head in a pale, dripping arc.

"You old fox," Bradley accused. "Don't try to pull that pitiful-old-lady stuff with me. You run three times a week, you can drink a longshoreman under the table, and I know you still carry a pearl-handled derringer in your purse.''

Amber heard a plopping sound and had a mental image of Bradley flinging himself into a plush, leather couch, peeling back the silver tab of his drink and gulping it—his long, muscular legs stretched casually out in front of him.

''Don't be rude, you horrible, ungrateful boy. You know I haven't been very well.''

There was a pause, then the groan of leather furniture as a heavy body shifted forward. ''What are you talking about? What's wrong?''

Amber held her breath. They were very close—just on the opposite side of the wall.

''Oh, well . . . ,'' Grandy said, her voice impatient. ''It's that new doctor. The quack. The way he keeps switching my pills you'd think I was some sort of lab rat.''

''If he does anything irresponsible, I'll make him sorry.''

Gooseflesh rose on Amber's arms. The anger communicated in those simple words was chilling. This was no threat. It was a promise.

''Well,'' Grandy snapped, ''if you really cared so damned much you'd do the simple thing I ask.''

''So my getting married is now the cure for high blood pressure?'' he said sarcastically.

''You know that's not what I mean. The company is in transition, and I'm worried sick about it. There's so much competition out there. You've seen what kind of dedication it takes to make this sort of thing work. You know your grandfather and I made this company our life.'' Her voice fell. ''Sometimes I think we may have sacrificed too much. We could have been better parents...'' She paused. ''But what's done is done. It's what Pope and I dedicated our lives to, and I'm afraid that when I'm gone there won't be anyone who gives a good—''

"You know that's not true. I've busted my tail for years."

"Yes, but the board won't trust you if you're not stable, will they? A thirty-one-year-old playboy is not exactly who the investors want for chairman of the—"

"Playboy? I'm not a playboy. I hardly play at all. I'm either here or at the ranch all the time. And since I don't have any interests outside the company, when the time comes I think the board'll decide I'm perfect."

Amber heard a snort of laughter. "Don't kid yourself," Grandy said. "These are old, traditional family people. You know they only trust their own kind. They want stability, and that means family commitment. Look at the board. Not one divorce amongst them, and you know how rotten half their marriages are. Just last week Ned Scarritt was saying he'd never trust a man who didn't have a family. I know these people, Bradley. I've worked with them for fifty years."

There was a stretch of silence. Amber glanced over her shoulder. She knew Zita would be coming back any moment, and she didn't want to be caught with her head almost sticking through the wall.

"I don't think you should work yourself into a state about this," Bradley said. His voice sounded suddenly tired. "Besides, if you have to know, I think I've found someone."

"Really? Why that's wonderful. Who is she?"

"I'm not ready to say, Grandy. I don't want to tell anyone just yet."

Amber heard a sigh of disgust, a hand falling softly on a table. "I see. You don't trust me."

There was another short stretch of silence during which Amber's heart thumped painfully and she fought incipient tears. He was on the verge of announcing his engagement to Tovah. Probably just because she was beautiful, rich and sophisticated and they had identical backgrounds and life-styles. Amber bit the inside of her lip. How shallow can you get?

"You can drop the guilt trip, Grandy. Others much better at it have failed."

"Oh, yes," she murmured. "How *is* your mother?"

Another pause ensued, and Amber could imagine them facing each other across an expanse of Persian rug, old sparring partners who obviously loved and respected each other.

"If you're going to be nasty, I'm leaving," he said.

"I'm sorry. You're right."

Amber heard the creak of an unoiled chair.

"So you've really found someone?"

"Can we talk about something else?"

Her heart rose. *He's squirming. That means he's not telling the truth. He's just trying to appease his grandmother.*

"Certainly not that walking cadaver you brought tonight."

"You've known Tovah all her life, Grandy."

"I've known her mother for forty-five years and I never could stand her."

There was no telling how much longer their conversation would last, Amber thought. It didn't matter. She'd heard all she needed to hear. Bradley Alan Ackerman was available and unattached. From the conversation she'd overheard she knew this was the time for him to settle down, and Amber was determined to make him see that she was the one he was meant to settle for. Or rather with. They were meant to be together. She'd never felt so sure about anything in her life.

She found a broom, cleaned up the floor and made several more trips to the tables. Although she was too elated to eat that night, the leftovers would make elegant lunches for the next few days.

Zita appeared, and together they bagged up everything that looked appetizing. When they walked past Bradley Ackerman's office later, the light shining under the door told them he was still there working, so Amber didn't have a chance to see his office. She wasn't disappointed in the least. She knew their time would come.

''Poor Amber,'' Scarlet said, patting her on the shoulder. ''Do you know the cause of these delusions? Have you suffered a closed head injury?''

Amber swatted at her younger sister with a wet dish towel. ''I should have known you'd scoff,'' she said. ''Well, you can scoff away, but I know what I know.''

Maude O'Reilly gave her middle daughter a pinched and worried look. ''Sweetheart, this really isn't like you. Are you sure that you're not suffering some kind of stress? I mean, with your new job and all those classes you're taking at school, is it too much, do you think?''

''No, Mama. All that's fine. My job's perfect, and I'm doing great in school. This is really love at first sight.''

Scarlet rolled her eyes, pointed at her temple and circled her finger in the universal sign that meant nutty. Amber gave her sister a frosty look. ''And I know he felt something, too.''

With the last of the lunch plates dried, she folded the dish towel and hung it over the rod by the kitchen window; the hot Gulf breeze lifted the thin cotton material and made it swing slightly. ''Besides, even if he doesn't realize it at first, I know I can make him notice me.''

She walked to the old linoleum table, scooted one of the chairs out and sat down and wound her ankles around the cool, tubular metal legs of the chair.

"When did all this happen, sweetheart?" Maude asked, and the fair skin on her forehead furrowed with worry.

"Two weeks ago." Amber frowned. "Actually I haven't seen him very much since. He usually leaves before I get there, and so far that's kind of a sticky point."

"Mama's right. This really isn't like you, Amber," Violet said. Violet, the oldest of Maude's daughters, sat thoughtfully at the other end of the table with her mother. She had washed the dishes so the other two girls had to dry.

Amber studied her oldest sister. You never really knew what Violet was thinking. She was a librarian, and of the three daughters she was the quiet, serious one. A river of heavy, midnight-dark hair hung down her back in a braid as thick as a hawser, and she was wearing one of her oversize flower-print dresses and plain loafers with socks. Antique, gold-rimmed glasses perched on the edge of her perfectly shaped nose. "You know we love you and we worry about you living all alone in Houston." She said *Houston* like some people say *toxic waste site.*

"Look, I'm fine. Everything's going great. I still come here almost every other weekend, and we all talk three or four times a week. Don't worry. This is happy news."

"It's just that you've never said anything like this before," Vi said softly.

"I know," Amber replied firmly. "That's why I'm sure it's real."

Scarlet sighed and cut an exasperated look at her mother and oldest sister. "I'll make the call," she said in a sarcastic stage whisper. She made a simpering smile at Amber. "You'll like the nice place where we're sending you—lots of arts and crafts, and soft food you won't even have to cut up."

Amber pursed her lips at her sister. Scarlet—beautiful Scarlet with her brains and bad temper. She was five-ten, thin as a rake and had modeled part of her way through college. Although a dozen agencies had been slobbering to sign her, she found the work boring, the people disgusting and the money simply not worth it. She quit, finished school on a basketball scholarship and now ran her own desktop publishing business.

Even dressed as she was now, wearing cutoffs and a Houston Cougars sweatshirt with the sleeves hacked out, she could easily have walked onto the cover shoot for a glossy fashion magazine. Except for maybe her hair. The beach air always played havoc with Scarlet's wiry red hair, and it now stood out from her head like a flaming, corkscrew sunburst.

Amber had often wished she had either of her sisters' dramatic looks: Scarlet had her striking model's face and figure, and Violet could have posed as a heroine for a medieval novel. Since they were really half sisters, Amber knew it wasn't unusual that the three of them shared little family resemblance. Still, she couldn't help but feel wistful something. She knew she resembled a cheerleader recruitment poster—blond, athletic and perky. No drama at all.

"I don't see what you're all in an uproar about," she said. "It's not like I'm inexperienced. I've had relationships."

"I'll say," Scarlet muttered.

"I heard that," Amber returned. "Now can you honestly say I've been foolish about men?"

"No," her mother replied thoughtfully. "To be honest, I suppose I'd have to say you've always shown good sense, but then again I can't think of anyone you ever dated that you were this enthusiastic about."

"Amber's Legion of the Lovelorn still meets at the house," Scarlet said, flinging her lanky frame into the fourth chair. She grabbed a nectarine from the wooden bowl in the center of the table and began to turn it in her hands. "Bobby Lucas came by last week."

Amber's jaw dropped. "You're kidding. I haven't seen Bobby in years."

"They all still come by," Scarlet said. "Just ask Mama. Or Daddo. They're the ones who spend hours mopping up the tears of unrequited love."

"Enough, Scarlet Marie," Maude said.

"At least *I* always end up friends with my former boyfriends," Amber retorted. "Anyway, what makes you think Bradley Ackerman won't be attracted to me?" She stood, and the legs of her chair made a sandy scraping noise across the floor. She poured more tea into her glass and scooped ice out of the freezer. Then, turning in a slow circle, she extended her arms demonstratively. "What's not to like? I'm young—"

"Oh, brother," Scarlet said, shaking her head.

"—well educated."

"You *have* been going to college for years," Violet murmured. "Although so far you've managed to avoid getting a degree."

"You know that's not my fault, Vi," Amber said. The words slipped out of her mouth, and for a moment she was afraid her mother might have misconstrued her meaning, but Maude just smiled at her serenely. "Not to mention the fact that I have a sunny disposition and an engaging personality—"

"Oh, barf," Scarlet muttered.

"—and I'm practically a virgin."

Both sisters hooted with laughter, and Maude gave them all motherly disapproving looks.

"What's going on in there?"

The booming, masculine voice of Liam O'Reilly rolled in from the deck. Amber opened the screen door.

"Your other daughters are abusing me, Daddo."

"Well, tell them to keep it down. I can't hear the game."

The four women passed looks at each other.

Amber walked back to the table and sat down. "How's he doing, Mama?"

Although Maude smiled, somehow the expression just made her look more worried. "The tests all say he's still in remission, and his hair is starting to come back." She shrugged and sighed. "We just take it a day at a time."

Scarlet leaned forward, and anxiety made deep grooves in her forehead. "He's doing everything he's supposed to, isn't he?"

"Mostly. He's impatient, that's all. He didn't want to retire, and he's frustrated because he feels so weak. And there are so many things he can't do."

Scarlet sat back. "So many things he can't smoke, you mean."

"I heard that," a gruff voice called from outside.

"You shouldn't eavesdrop," Scarlet yelled.

Amber felt a twinge of conscience. The word *eavesdrop* reminded her of the conversation she'd deliberately overheard. She glanced at her watch. "Well, I hate leaving you all here, but I'd better head back if I'm going to get to work on time. It's one o'clock now, and I want to run by the house before I go to the office. How long are you all planning on staying?"

"Well," Maude said, "we're not on a timetable."

"I'm staying until Sunday," Scarlet said. "Vi's driving me home."

The old house at Crystal Beach was their favorite family gathering place—a sprawling story and a half raised on piers facing the Gulf of Mexico. Daddo had owned it before he married Maude and used to bring her down when they were courting.

"Well," Amber said, "I'd better fly." After a round of noisy hugs and kisses, she gathered up her sandy things, threw them into the back of the Toyota and went bouncing down the powdery beach road toward the highway back to Houston.

"Are you out of your mind? Why the hell would we need two hundred thousand dollars' worth of ten-foot chain-link fence?" Bradley had been at the ranch for only moments; he'd thrown his coat and briefcase down on the table in the flagstone foyer and walked into the den to find his father on the phone, bragging to one of his cronies about the fence he'd ordered.

Phillip saluted Bradley with a lift of his heavy crystal highball glass, dropped the phone into the cradle then turned to his son and pulled a face of mock anguish. "But I'm doing it all for us. Ah, 'How sharper than a serpent's tooth it is to have a thankless child.'" He drummed his thin lips with his fingers. "That's *Hamlet*, isn't it?"

"*King Lear,*" Bradley snapped. "What the hell are you thinking of? That's the budget for the ranch for four years. This won't be approved and you know it."

"I approved it myself," Phillip said. "Of course, if my dear, old, gray-haired mammy refuses to pay, I guess I'll just have to see your mother, my meek and long-suffering wife."

A familiar clutch of helpless fury took Bradley by the middle. If the family corporation did not pay for what Phillip wanted, he would take more money from Blanche, who adored her husband helplessly and would allow him to eventually bleed every dollar from her trust.

Bradley eyed his father and fought a wave of disgust and despair. His heart had sunk the minute he'd driven up and seen Phillip's Rolls skewed across the driveway. He tried to remember everything he'd learned about keeping his temper in check. "So exactly why do you want a ten-foot chain-link fence?"

"To keep in the exotic game. The axis deer, gemsbok *and*—" he swept his arm grandly "—the teeming herds of wildebeast my friends and I will be shooting."

The pain in Bradley's gut ratcheted up a notch. "You're not turning Pope's ranch into a weekend slaughterhouse for you and—"

"Pope's ranch? Pope's ranch is it? I seem to remember the old bastard dying about fifteen years ago."

"Don't talk about him like that, Dad."

Phillip poured another two fingers of Scotch into his glass. "You know what your problem is, Bradley? You're not a father. Unless you're keeping a secret somewhere." He leered. "Which wouldn't surprise me in the least. After all, you're a true Ackerman, and we all know the apple doesn't fall too far from the tree, does it? Once you have a family of your own, you'll understand the affection that grows between a father and his son."

"How long are you staying?"

Phillip shrugged. "Haven't decided. Oh, I hope I haven't messed anything up for you. You weren't planning to bring Ella Stein's bony daughter here, were you? This could be interesting. I think she likes me."

Bradley felt himself turn cold. "Don't say another word about her or any of my friends again," he said quietly. Something in his tone must have registered, because Phillip stopped for a moment before the animosity in his eyes turned to something even more bitter.

"What's the matter, son? Don't you want to be a true Ackerman? Don't you think there's such a thing as destiny?"

"I hope not."

In the quiet that followed, Bradley heard the ticking of the clock, the grating cry of a blue jay and the distant creaks and groans of the old house settling in the withering heat.

"Well, did you ever think that maybe your old dad's just not the brilliant businessman you are?" The corner of the older man's mouth curled, and he took a long drink from his glass. He grinned and crunched the ice in his mouth. His reddish hair had thinned over the years, and he had a high, aristocratic forehead and handsome if cruel features. His green eyes were a little glazed with the Scotch he had obviously been pouring himself all afternoon.

"You can cut the crap, Dad. I know what you're doing. You're deliberately trying to destroy this ranch. And if they make you chairman, you'll run the company into the ground, too."

Phillip staggered in mock horror and clutched dramatically at his chest. He'd taken off his jacket, and his sleeves were rolled up to reveal the fair skin grizzled with coarse red-blond hair. "You wound me, Bradley. Now why on earth would I want to do that? Squander the family legacy? Stumble rather than walk proudly in my father's gigantic footsteps?"

As he spoke, Phillip made a grand flourish with his glass and sloshed dark liquid onto the black enameled surface of Grandy's concert piano. He regarded it with a look of perverse satisfaction.

Bradley eyed him coldly. "You'd do it because you know I love this ranch more than anyplace else in the world, and the company was the most important thing in Pope's life." He took a napkin from the bar, walked to the piano and cleaned up his father's mess. This brought them face-to-face. "And you hated him, you hate the company, and you hate me." These facts were enumerated dispassionately.

Phillip Ackerman returned his son's gaze, and for a fleeting instant Bradley saw the flash of pain. Or was it supposed to be contrition? Bradley didn't soften his expression. After years of falling for this ploy, he'd learned his lesson.

Besides, he knew what he said was true, but these truths had long ago lost their power to hurt him. He also realized this made his father even more bitter and frustrated.

Bradley's eyes never left his father's, and Phillip threw his arms wide in an extravagant gesture. "Now why wouldn't I adore my dear old dad?"

"Because he didn't have time for you. Because he was ashamed of you—"

Phillip winced. He had, as usual, cornered his son and picked this quarrel but, as always, he seemed genuinely amazed when Bradley fought back.

Brad unclenched his fists and rolled his shoulders. He hated this feeling of helpless fury. Despite countless promises to Grandy and his mother, he was often drawn into these bitter exchanges. He never quite understood how his father managed so effectively to goad him when he was already on guard.

Despite all his good intentions, fifteen minutes in Phillip's company—especially if the older man was drinking—turned Bradley back into a furious, red-faced, twelve-year-old trying to fend off an antagonist who was older, more experienced and much, much more vicious.

"But he had plenty of time when you came along didn't he," Phillip said in a low, tight voice. "All you had to do was show up and Pope Ackerman turned into Grandpa Walton, dispensing time and nuggets of homey wisdom—"

"And the attention you never did."

Phillip let himself fall back into one of the hide-covered, horsehair sofas. He grinned. "Hand me my violin, oh, fruit of my loins."

Bradley turned on his heel and walked toward the arched door. *The only way to win is not to play.* He repeated the familiar mantra the same way he had countless times before. He had intended to spend the weekend riding the fence line and fishing with the Graftons. He felt the tendon in his jaw popping. He shouldn't have told anyone where he was going. No doubt his doting dad had found out the plan and dropped everything to race to the hill country to indulge in his idea of father-son bonding.

Bradley's boot heels slammed through the stone entryway, and he grabbed up his briefcase from the antique claw-footed table. He'd just spent three hours driving up from Houston, and after fifteen minutes in Phillip's company, he was prepared to turn around and drive right back. Six hours in one day on Interstate 10 was a far more attractive proposition than a drunken evening with his father.

Bradley managed to slow his steps when he reached the door. He had no intention of giving Phillip the satisfaction of a loud, infuriated exit. When the phone rang he was tempted to ignore it, but at the last minute he turned and snatched the receiver out of the cradle. "Ackerman," he snapped.

"Brad, is that you?"

The voice was tentative and frightened.

"Spencer? Yeah, what's wrong?"

"It's Estelle . . ."

Bradley felt a cold hand reach into his chest and squeeze. "What's wrong with Grandy?"

Spencer Bailey was obviously fighting tears, and this terrified Bradley. Bailey was a lion of a man—statesmanlike and cool in the most dire of straits. He was as unflappable in a crisis as a combat wing commander, which he had been in World War II.

"Spence, what the hell is going on?"

"She's had an attack, Brad. A bad one, I think."

"Where is she?"

"EMS is here and they're working on her in her office. I'm going with them to the hospital, but I think you should come. Can you get a charter?"

"I don't know. Austin's an hour from here." His mind raced. What would take less time? Austin traffic and trying to charter a flight or . . . ? "I'm going to drive it. I'm leaving right now."

He set the receiver back down and hesitated in the entryway. Should he tell his father? He sure as hell had no intention of driving Phillip and his Scotch bottle all the way to Houston. But could he live with himself if he walked out without saying a word? What if something happened to Grandy? Phillip needed to know. He was, despite everything, her oldest son.

Cursing violently but quietly, Bradley steadied himself and walked back through to the den. Phillip stood at the bar stirring the ice in his glass with his index finger.

"That was Spence. They think Grandy's had a heart attack. She's at the office, but there's an ambulance there now. I'm driving back." The startled look on his father's face knifed through him. *Maybe he does care.* Bradley was about to offer to make a thermos of coffee for the drive back when Phillip snapped himself upright.

He first sucked the Scotch off his finger with a flourish, then swept his arms wide and then began to slap his hands together in loud, measured claps. "Bradley the Boy Wonder to the rescue."

The door rattled on its hinges when Bradley slammed it shut.

Chapter Three

Amber sang all the words she remembered of "Just One Look" as she rinsed the salty film off her truck. The days she'd spent at the beach had been both relaxing and restorative. She'd gone fishing and crabbing with her sisters, shamelessly lazed around reading gossipy magazines and summer novels and she'd eaten whatever she wanted. Since she'd been a little careless about using sunscreen, her skin had bronzed while her dishwater blond hair had bleached in streaks to a pale flax.

She felt so replete and content, she didn't really even mind having to go to work on Friday afternoon—the time when most people were just starting their weekends. When she finished washing the truck, she unpacked her bags, sorted her mail and did a couple of loads of laundry. Then there was nothing left to do but get ready for work.

After showering, she decided to wear something cool and feminine to the office, so she chose a yellow sundress and strappy sandals with thick cork soles. She even decided to forego her customary ponytail, and her loose hair fell in a straight, heavy pageboy just past her shoulders.

Amber wasn't vain, but she knew she looked about as good as she ever could—tanned, rested and happy. She smiled a little ruefully at her reflection.

"This is exactly how you look," she said, "when no one important sees you."

Thirty minutes later when she pulled into Ackerman, she wasn't surprised at all to see that the garage was almost completely deserted. What did surprise her and cause a tiny hitch in her breath was the long, black, eight-cylinder Fiugioli parked in the executive slot next to the entrance.

It was Bradley's. Amber had done more than a little judicious asking around in the last two weeks, and Zita, with an I-hope-you-know-what-you're-doing look, had told her everything she knew.

Amber had just swung wide, intending to take the slot adjoining Bradley's car when she heard the grinding—a tortured, mechanical growl that grew deeper and more tired with every rotation, like the sound of a giant toy slowly winding down. Then the driver's side door flew open and Bradley jumped out, his expression livid.

With a look of murderous frustration he slammed the door, then turned and his gaze connected with Amber's. Without a moment's hesitation he strode toward the truck.

"This is an emergency," he said, and his voice was shockingly composed. "Can you drive me to the hospital right now?"

Of course. Anywhere.

Amber said, "Yes. Get in."

"Thanks."

He sprinted around the front of the truck and was halfway to the other side when Amber moved the gearshift into

Park and opened the door. "If you know the way, why don't you drive?"

Bradley slid to a stop, nodded and headed for the driver's side. By the time Amber had unbuckled her seat belt and scooted across the vinyl bench seat, he already had his hands on the steering wheel. He was just reaching to put the truck in gear when he cursed, shouldered the door open again and jumped out. "I forgot something. Just a second."

He ran to his car, yanked open the door and leaned inside. When he came back, he handed her a sport coat and a book. Amber took them wordlessly.

Bradley threw the pickup into reverse before he even had the door shut, and the Toyota leapt backward, throwing Amber against her shoulder harness.

"Sorry," he said, and glanced quickly at her as he whipped the truck into an empty parking place. "Are you okay? I'm sorry," he said again, and then nodded at the book in Amber's lap. "That's my grandfather's Bible."

He slammed the gearshift into drive and burned rubber toward the exit. "Grandy—my grandmother—is in ICU at Burdyne Memorial. That Bible is the one thing she asked for. I keep it in my safe, so I had to stop and get it. No one else has the combination."

From his distracted tone Amber wasn't sure if he was talking to her or himself. For that matter she wasn't sure if he even recognized her.

"Your grandmother is sick?"

He nodded. "They took her to ICU sometime this afternoon. It's her heart."

In moments Amber's own heart was thundering. For one thing, Bradley Ackerman now sat less than two feet away, but even more harrowing than that, he had plowed into the Houston rush hour traffic as if he were competing in a demolition derby. Horns blared, drivers gesticulated furiously, and Amber shrank deep into her seat and braced herself for the impending, inevitable crash.

Bradley dodged across the lanes. "I didn't want to go back to the office," he said, taking one hand off the steering wheel to make a helpless gesture. Amber, goggle-eyed, pointed at the cars swirling and slewing around them. "Spence called me on the car phone, and he told me the one time she regained consciousness she asked for Pope's Bible. What was I supposed to do? I had to stop and get it, and then that damned forty-thousand-dollar piece of..."

His voiced trailed off into vile expletives. "The damned car wouldn't start again." His free hand once again slammed back into a choke on the steering wheel. Amber felt marginally safer.

She hoped the hospital wasn't too far away. She thought it was just down Richmond, but despite geographical proximity, dozens of traffic lights separated Burdyne Memorial and the Ackerman Drilling office. Bradley ran every one he could, but if both lanes of cars in front of him stopped he had no choice but to stop behind them, cursing under his breath and checking his watch while the seconds ticked past.

Amber understood and sympathized with his desperation, although the illness her stepfather was suffering from had been slow and agonizing rather than sudden and critical.

Traffic still crawled sluggishly between the lights, and although Bradley didn't say more, his palpable fear filled the small, enclosed space until Amber felt it might suffocate them both. She could read the naked anguish on his face. *Is she still alive? Will I get to say goodbye?*

As they struggled to maneuver through the traffic, Amber thought there seemed to be an almost diabolical intent to keep them from their destination. She soon saw the reason—the unmistakable strobe of patrol car lights far ahead. In moments both westbound lanes came to a complete stop. Rising above the treetops in the distance beyond a gentle curve in the road, Amber could see the upper stories of Burdyne Memorial. She knew Bradley saw it, too.

He clutched the steering wheel, and his knuckles stood up painfully white against his dark skin. He didn't curse aloud, but Amber could almost hear the violent language of his thoughts. He looked over at her. "I can't just sit here. I've got to—"

"Go," Amber urged. "It's not that far."

He nodded, put the truck in park and popped the door latch, then grabbed up the old Bible and stepped out. At the last moment he turned and pushed the door shut carefully. "Thanks," he said.

Amber nodded and smiled encouragement to him, and he turned and waded into the blazing, white-hot afternoon. She saw him dodge between the stalled cars and up onto the grass median separating the eastbound and westbound lanes. The moment his feet hit the grass, he broke into a run and was soon far away.

Amber let her arms relax and realized, moments too late, that what she'd been clutching to her chest was Bradley's jacket. Almost reflexively she lifted it, "You forgot your—" she murmured at the disappearing figure.

Far ahead she saw him stop, hop in place for a moment, then sprint across the lanes of oncoming traffic and up onto the sidewalk. She took a breath, unbuckled herself and slid back into the driver's seat.

Her thoughts tumbled all the way back to the office. She wondered if there was anything else she could do to help him or his family. Probably not. She should have offered, she thought, but then again, he was so obviously distraught, he probably didn't even remember who she was.

Amber thought of Estelle Ackerman and had a momentary sense of loss that she hadn't had the chance to get to know that remarkable woman. But maybe, she hoped, Bradley's grandmother would recover. Amber quickly sent up a few of what her mother called "foxhole prayers."

When she pulled into the parking lot for the second time that day, she decided she'd just leave Bradley's jacket on the chair in his office. Once the elevator doors closed and she felt safely out of sight, she slung the coat over her shoulders and let herself be swallowed in it.

The feeling was at once exhilarating and intimate. A ghost of his after-shave—pine and leather—lingered elusively in the smooth lining. Amber decided to allow herself one further indulgence. She slipped her arms into the sleeves and hugged herself . . . and felt a solid little rectangle in the breast pocket.

His wallet.

"Oh, no," she murmured as she took it out. With only a moment's hesitation she flipped it open, noted the typically unflattering Texas Department of Public Safety photograph on his license, and instantly committed his birthday—September third—to memory. *Is that Leo? No, Virgo.* Facing his license was a platinum card, and then Amber noted with a rise of horror, the unmistakable corner of a crisp one-hundred-dollar bill. She felt an anguished moment of guilt for even looking.

She decided if there was a fair amount of money in the billfold she would hide the wallet somewhere in his office and leave a message for him at the ICU nurse's station. But if there was *more* than a fair amount . . .

There was more than a fair amount. There was a frightening amount. Bradley had more money in his wallet than

Amber took home in a month. She rode the elevator back down, stopped in and told Zita where she'd been and where she was going. Then she took the elevator back to the garage and headed, once again, toward Burdyne Memorial.

The first person she saw, sitting alone on a narrow bench in the hallway outside the ICU, was Spencer Bailey. His appearance shocked her. He looked crumpled and too small for his clothes and very, very old. He was resting his face in his palms, and his elbows were digging into his knees. Amber thought immediately that he had old-man hands—blue veined and liver spotted with knuckles overlarge and painfully arthritic looking.

"Mr. Bailey?"

He looked up, and the desolation in his face struck her like a physical blow, but he immediately pulled himself erect and stood. A gentleman, she thought, even in the most terrible of times. "Yes?"

"I'm Amber Oakland...from the office. I dropped Bradley off a little while ago."

"He's with his grandmother right now."

Clipped consonants and perfect enunciation were the only traces of his British accent. Nearly fifty years in Texas had smoothed away the rest.

Oh, God, surely she's not...

"He left his jacket in the car. With his wallet."

Spencer Bailey blinked slowly, almost painfully as he visibly tried to assimilate what she said. "Thank you so much for your trouble, Miss Oakland. I don't think he'll be too long, but if you don't care to wait, I'll see that he gets it."

Amber hesitated and wondered if she should go or sit with him. She hated to leave him there all by himself; he looked so alone. She wondered if she should offer to stay or help, but even before she said the words they seemed pathetically trite and meaningless. *If there's anything I can do to help, please feel free . . .*

There was nothing anyone could do. Amber had kept this vigil herself—sleeping on hard, plastic waiting room furniture or not sleeping at all. She'd lived on food from vending machines, too terrified to go home to shower or sleep for fear that something would happen to her father while she was gone, and knowing that she would have to live the rest of her life hating herself for not being there.

She understood firsthand the terrible helplessness of praying and promising and knowing all the while that one of the candles in your life is in the next room slowly burning out.

In these times you didn't ask, you acted. "I'm going down for some coffee," she said. "Would you like a cup or would you prefer tea?"

He almost sagged with gratitude, and Amber had to swallow more than once to keep her eyes from filling.

"A cup of tea," he said, "would be . . . would—"

"I'll be right back."

She bought coffee for herself and Bradley and tea for Mr. Bailey, and when she returned she saw them standing head-to-head just outside the ICU door. The older man had his back to her and didn't see her coming.

". . . can't lose her, Brad," he said, in a ravaged voice. "I don't think I could live if she were gone."

Amber suddenly recalled the photographs in his office—the stunning young woman in front of the pyramids, the coquette posed in the jet intake. She wondered if Grandy meant even more to Spencer Bailey than a dear friend and lifetime business associate.

Had Spencer Bailey been in love with Estelle Ackerman all these years? She'd heard that he'd never married and now she wondered if this was the explanation.

How sad for him, she thought. How sad for anyone to spend a whole life loving someone and to never have that love returned.

One thing she was certain of though; he wouldn't want her to see how disordered he was by his grief.

"Here we are," she said briskly.

Bradley had slipped his jacket on, and when he saw her he tried to smile. "Hello again. Thanks for coming all the way back to bring me this. I'm afraid I was out of my head."

"Of course," she said. "Here's your tea, Mr. Bailey. I brought sugar and lemon, too." She turned to Bradley. "Do you want some coffee? I brought extra."

"Thanks," he said, and gratefully took the extra cup from her. "I don't know how I'm going to ever pay you back for everything you've done for me today."

Amber's cheeks flamed, and she hoped she wasn't blushing. "I'm happy to help," she said.

Just as Amber started to excuse herself, he turned toward Spencer. "What time are Uncle Theron and Uncle Moe supposed to get here?"

The older man checked his watch. "They should have landed about twenty minutes ago. Suzette can't come. Her doctor's afraid to let her get too far away because of the trouble she's having. Adele can't get a flight out until tomorrow."

Zita had told Amber that Bradley had two sisters: Suzette, a Dallas socialite whose first baby was due within a couple of months, and Adele, an artist who lived somewhere on the West Coast. Theron and Moe were Phillip Ackerman's younger brothers, and Amber briefly wondered where Grandy's eldest son was. How horrible it would be for him, she thought, if he were somewhere and couldn't be found.

The gossip she'd heard flashed through her mind along with the ugly thought that he might be somewhere with another woman. What if something happened to his mother and no one could find him? She almost shuddered; the burden of guilt would be insupportable.

"Who's going to the airport?" Brad asked.

Spencer's expression didn't change. "Your mother. She left just before you arrived."

Bradley's eyes grew hard.

"There was no one else," Spencer said quietly. "Besides, I was here and she needed to get out of here and go get the house ready for . . . company."

At that moment the ICU door opened and a nurse in green scrubs walked up to Bradley, her face composed but stern. "Mr. Ackerman, your grandmother is asking for you."

Fear and hope both flashed across his face, but he didn't say anything. He turned, obviously looking for someplace to set down his cup. Amber took it, and then he disappeared through the door.

Spencer Bailey looked more haggard than ever. Amber wondered if he was hurt that Grandy hadn't asked for him. No, she thought, he's just worrying himself sick. She didn't want to intrude in his private anguish, but she certainly wasn't going to leave him there all by himself. She would wait until more of Bradley's family arrived, then she'd slip out. She crossed the hall, sat on the narrow bench and sipped her coffee. After only a moment's hesitation he joined her.

"What does Mrs. Ackerman's doctor say?" she asked.

The corners of his mouth turned down. "We can't find him. The hospital staff has been paging him, and the doctor on call hasn't been very forthcoming, either. He tells us that all the tests they've done so far are inconclusive."

Amber remembered what Bradley had told his grandmother about her doctor. *If he does anything irresponsible, I'll make him sorry.* She didn't doubt for a second that he would make good on that promise.

Amber was about to make another attempt at conversation when the ICU door flew open and Bradley appeared, looking almost frantic. Spencer stood.

"What is it?"

"She's conscious, but she's really upset," he said. "It's my fault. I did something stupid, and now she . . ." Bradley's voice trailed off, and Amber could see that he had suddenly noticed her, but she couldn't tell what he was thinking. He hesitated just a minute, then walked up to where she was sitting.

"I have to ask you for a favor," he said. "A big one."

"What can I do to help?"

Bradley shifted uncomfortably. "Will you be my fiancée?"

"What?"

"I'm sorry. There isn't much time to explain, but my grandmother thinks I'm engaged."

Oh, yes, Amber thought, that conversation she'd eavesdropped on a couple of weeks ago. *I think I've found someone,* he'd said. She knew he wasn't telling the truth.

Bradley glanced back toward the doors. "She's convinced herself that she's not going to make it, and she wants to meet the person I'm going to marry before she..." Bradley swallowed and gave Spence a stricken look. "She's worked herself into a state. She pulled the IV out of her hand." He shook his head. "I never meant to—"

"I'll do it," Amber said. "Just tell me what you want me to say."

Bradley, obviously relieved, backed toward the door. "Just…I don't know. It won't be much. We can only stay with her for a minute, anyway."

Amber dropped her purse on the bench and gave Spencer what she hoped was a comforting smile. She didn't feel the least bit hesitant over what she was about to do. Grandy was dying. She just wanted to meet the girl that her much-loved grandson was going to marry. Such a little thing, Amber thought, such a tiny white lie, to make a dying woman happy.

Bradley led her down a short corridor. All around them the air shimmered with controlled urgency, the crisp comings and goings of nurses in quiet concentration, the hiss and crackle of critical care technology with all its desperate imperatives.

No one took much notice of them, and Amber wondered how Bradley was allowed such access. She would have asked, but there wasn't time. He touched her arm and she tipped her face up.

They stood so close she could see the burrs of color in his eyes, and the fine pattern of lines just beneath his eyelashes. He didn't say anything right away, and for a moment Amber thought he might be having second thoughts. "I'm sorry," he said. He blinked and to Amber it seemed that she had only, that very moment, come into focus for him. She saw something different in his look, something that said he had only just recognized her.

"I'm sorry," he said again. "Please forgive me, but I don't remember your name."

She smiled a little. "It's Amber. Amber Oakland."

He winced. "Of course, Amber. I'm sorry. It's just all this—"

He encompassed everything around them, including his own desperation, with a lift of his hands.

"It's okay," she said. "I know exactly how you feel."

He smiled his gratitude, then took her elbow and led her into one of the alcoves.

Estelle Ackerman lay on her back, and a clear tube feeding her oxygen circled her face and pressed into her pale cheeks. Ruined makeup stained her eyelids, and her pretty silver hair lay matted against the starched cotton pillowcase. Amber was surprised at how small a woman she was; from her portrait and her voice, Amber had expected someone tall—a pioneer type. She had envisioned a rawboned but stately woman, not this tiny stick figure wired and dwarfed by the size of the bed and the trailing machinery that clicked and chugged along, dutifully occupied with keeping her alive.

Paper-thin eyelids fluttered open, and Estelle Ackerman looked up at her grandson, then her gaze tilted over to Amber. She didn't speak, but the tiniest lift of her finger beckoned them closer. Amber moved to the bed.

Bradley's voice was tender. "This is Amber, Grandy. Amber, this is my grandmother, Estelle Ackerman."

"Hello, Mrs. Ackerman," Amber said, and gently touched the thin arm. Skin and bones, she thought, but there still seemed to be strength there. "I'm glad to finally meet you. I'm sorry you're not feeling very well."

Pale, dry lips pulled into a smile. Her mouth moved to form her grandson's name, and her hummingbird chest rose and fell with effort that was painful to watch. With the slightest move of her hand, she patted the bed beside her, motioning Amber to sit.

Amber turned to Bradley and let her eyes ask the question. *Do you think this is all right?* He nodded, and Amber thought she saw a sheen in his eyes.

"Tell me . . ." the tiny woman whispered, "tell me your full name."

"Amber Louise Oakland."

"Amber Louise," the old woman said, and smiled. "My middle name is Louise, too."

"Bradley told me," she lied.

"You're very pretty."

"Thank you." *What can I say? How can I make her happy?*

The thin breath hitched suddenly and the older woman winced; Amber cast a fearful look at Bradley, and he leaned closer. "Grandy, are you okay? Shall I get the doctor?"

"Oh, don't fuss, Bradley," she said, and her voice grew stronger with irritation. "I just can't stand all these gewgaws poking into me." The effort of speech obviously taxed her, and she lay still for a moment with her eyes closed, panting quietly.

When Amber tried to slide quietly up, the fierce little blue gaze stopped her. "Don't go. I want you to tell me—" she paused to catch her breath "—tell me what you love the most about my grandson."

Amber did her best to keep her eyes from widening in panic. Being cornered this way was unexpected, and she heard Bradley shifting uncomfortably beside her. *What do I love the most about him?* Well, she thought, at least I don't have to invent much. Everything she'd learned about him had only deepened her conviction that he was a fine and decent man—just the one for her. But one thing for certain, no matter what she was trying to do, she couldn't mention how she'd felt the moment she'd first seen him.

"I guess," she began and smiled a little, "I guess the first thing I noticed was his mind. He's so smart, and he works so hard—too hard, I think sometimes. And then there's his dry sense of humor."

She swallowed and hoped Bradley would think that she was just making up what she thought Grandy might want to hear. Maybe he would assume that her litany of his virtues was nothing but well-meaning prevarication recited for the benefit of a dying woman. But what if he heard the truth in her voice and realized what she was saying was how she truly felt about him? Unfortunately, nothing could be done about that right now.

"But I think," she said softly, "what moves me the most is the way he takes care of the people he loves. How could any woman not love that?"

Grandy's eyes closed and one thin tear slipped over her powdered cheek. "I knew it," she whispered. "The moment I saw you, I had a feeling that you were the one." Her smile finally reached her eyes. "Do you know what I mean?"

Amber nodded. "I know exactly what you mean."

She wiped her own cheek with the back of her hand and stood. If she didn't leave now, she'd burst into tears. "I'll come back and we'll talk more when you're feeling better," Amber said softly, her voice husky with unshed tears.

Grandy's eyes met hers, and there was no mistaking the message in the old woman's look. *We both know that's not going to happen.*

As she backed toward the door, Grandy raised her hand in a feeble wave. Then she turned to her grandson. "Bradley," she whispered, "kiss her goodbye."

"What?"

"I want to see you kiss her," she said, her face pleading.

Amber faced Bradley and knew his look must have matched the one she had earlier—incredulity mixed liberally with guilt and a dash of panic.

"I..." he began. "I—"

"What's the matter?" Grandy asked, her voice thin and weak. "Surely you've kissed her before. Pretty soon you're going to do it in front of a church full of people." She swallowed, visibly weakening. "But I won't be there to see it."

Bradley turned to Amber, his eyes communicating frantically. *I'm sorry about this, but it has to be believable.*

Then he faced her squarely, leaned down and pressed his lips to hers. Amber knew that he'd intended a gentle kiss, tender, but without passion—just something to convince his grandmother that this was indeed the woman he'd chosen to marry. For Amber, however, even despite the tragic circumstances, this was her first—maybe her only—kiss with the man of her dreams. She closed her eyes.

His mouth was warm and firm, and his hand on her shoulder was more reassuring than affectionate, but only seconds after his lips met hers Amber felt the change. She felt the surprise quiver through him as she poured her feelings into him through the touch of their mouths.

His hand slid under her hair and behind her neck, and she parted her lips slightly, her tongue grazing his. A shudder went through his body, and then she felt something letting go in him, the clenched tightness of hours spent fearfully and frantically. She knew he was taking comfort from everything she offered and accepting all of it—her comfort, sympathy, her tenderness.

And in that same moment she felt a distant stirring. The touch of his mouth and fingers told her that here was a powerful and passionate lover, here was a floodgate just waiting for the right hand to release an overwhelming tide. She sighed into his mouth, and his fingers eased up into her hair. The room receded and went spinning away, and just as Amber was reaching up to wind her arms around his neck, there was a confusion of voices in the hallway behind her.

The spell broke, and Bradley pulled away and stepped back. Amber dropped her eyes and cleared her throat. She knew her face would be scarlet and she was afraid to meet his eyes. She feared that the kiss had told him too much, and so instead of facing him, she turned back to his grandmother.

Grandy's eyes had drifted shut, but she was smiling.

A nurse appeared at the doorway. "Your family is here, Mr. Ackerman," she said.

Amber leaned over and kissed the soft, cool cheek. "Goodbye, Grandy," she whispered. "I'll come back soon."

There was no reply, and Amber turned and followed Bradley out of the alcove and back down the short corridor. They didn't speak.

Waiting in the hallway with Spencer was a petite, impeccably dressed and coiffed woman and two tall, middle-aged men. As soon as Bradley opened the door the woman practically threw herself into his arms. "Oh, Bradley," she said, her soft voice quavering with emotion. "Isn't it just too tragic? However will we all bear it?"

"Hello, Mama," he said, his voice even more tired than before.

Bradley's mother was a debutante from Birmingham, and more than thirty years in Texas hadn't made the slightest dent in her accent. She was a pretty, fluttery little woman, with small, manicured hands in constant motion, like birds who find themselves suddenly trapped.

"Why, honey," she said, her voice wobbling with incipient tears, "you just look exhausted. My poor darling. Have the doctors given us even the tiniest shred of hope?"

"She's holding her own right now," he answered, then he turned slightly, and Blanche obviously realized that Amber had been with him. Her hazel eyes measured surprise and curiosity.

"Mother," he said, "this is Amber, a friend of mine from the office. Amber, my mother, Blanche Ackerman. And these are my uncles, Theron and Morris."

There were polite murmurings and handshakes, and Bradley began telling them everything he knew about Grandy's condition. Amber slipped over to the hallway bench, picked up her purse and edged away. She had done all she could do, and there was no further reason for her to be there. This was a family time.

When she caught Bradley's eye, she pointed toward the door and mouthed the words, "I'll talk to you later."

He excused himself and walked over to her. "You were my angel today," he said. "I can't thank you enough for everything you did for all of us . . . for her."

Shyness overwhelmed her. Her mouth still tingled from the kiss, and she needed time to be alone and think about what had happened.

"Bradley," his mother called, "are we allowed to go in and see her?"

He turned back to them, and Amber left. She knew he had urgent concerns and the best way for her to help was to leave right then and not burden him further with the necessity of politeness or gratitude.

Just before stepping on the elevator she glanced back and saw Spencer staring after her. He looked thoughtful, but there was something else, too. Just as the doors closed, Amber was sure she saw a smile of satisfaction flit across his tired features.

Chapter Four

When Amber walked into the night staff office Zita looked up, her expression grave. "How is she?"

"I don't know. She seemed awfully weak, and the family's gathering. It doesn't look very good."

"What did her doctor say?"

Amber sat down. "This is really bad. They can't find him. Apparently the hospital's been paging him, but so far he hasn't called back. Bradley's furious."

Zita raised her brows. "Who wouldn't be?"

She gave Amber a thoughtful look. "You have the funniest expression on your face. Is something the matter?"

Amber told her what had happened, but for some reason she decided to leave out the kiss. The kiss she would save for herself and keep hidden like a stolen jewel to be taken out and cherished in more private moments.

Zita sat quietly until Amber finished her story. "Do you think she believed you? I mean, didn't she ask how you just happened to be waiting in the hallway?"

"I guess Bradley told her we were together when she got sick. Or maybe she was so out of it, she didn't think to ask." Amber thought for a moment. "Although she really didn't seem to be delirious." She shrugged. "Anyway, she believed us."

"What did the rest of the family say?"

"No one else knows. Only me and Bradley. Well, and Mr. Bailey. He was standing right there when Brad asked me to do it."

They sat in thoughtful silence for a moment, and Amber toyed with the pens on Zita's desk. "I wonder what this means for the company."

Zita rolled her eyes. "Probably chaos. We're in the middle of trying to get new contracts in South America, Grandy's been chairman ever since Pope died, and there are all sorts of warring factions on the board. Just you watch. First everything will come to a complete standstill, then all hell's gonna break loose."

She pointed an accusing finger at the In box. Empty.

At that moment the phone rang, and Amber went back to her cubicle and switched on her computer. Since there was no word processing to do, she decided to work on the history paper that was due in two weeks, but she couldn't seem to concentrate on President McKinley and the triumph of the Hamiltonian ideal.

Instead, she thought about the memory of the kiss. How had his mouth felt against hers? Amber pressed her fingers against her lips and closed her eyes. Remember the way he became suddenly aware of what was happening, she thought, the way his body suddenly relaxed toward hers. The way his fingers searched up into her hair? Their tongues had grazed. Had he sighed into her mouth or had she just imagined that?

Now he knows, too, she thought. Surely this was meant to be. Giddy hope took her imagination, and she began picking out china patterns and middle names for her children. The young, newly married Ackermans would work tirelessly side by side in education and the arts. In between ribbon cuttings and dedications, they would vacation in sandy, sunny places, drink fruity drinks decorated with umbrellas and massage tropical oils into each other's shoulders. And backs. And . . .

"Amber?"

The fantasy bubble popped and Amber jumped slightly. "Sorry," she said, looking up at Tam's confused expression. "I was just, em . . ."

Tam's eyes were sympathetic. "Praying. I can see that. I'm sorry to disturb you, but everyone's talking about it. Did you really have to take Brad to the hospital? How did that happen? And how's Mrs. Ackerman?"

The story had to be told again. Several times. Almost half of the clerical and professional staff had lingered long after it was time to go home and were drifting like unmoored boats from office to office. Quiet murmuring and speculation about the condition of the chairman echoed softly and plaintively in the hallways.

Amber heard the story of how Pope had died, also of a heart ailment, fifteen years earlier—too many steaks and brandies and not enough exercise. He had been a bear of a man—loud, bluff and often ruled by extravagant emotions. He was temperamental, generous and demanding, they said, and as dangerous as a cornered cur if threatened. Grandy had been with him every step of the way through the thirties and forties, forging an international oil field supply house out of a Texas wildcat drilling company. When Pope died, there was no question that she would be the one to take over the reins, but things had become more complicated in the ensuing years.

The international oil patch had become a tricky place to do business, the world had become small and competitive, and the choice of a future chairman became blurred by personal interests and company politics. Amber even heard some speculation about the prickly relationships between Phillip Ackerman, his son and his mother. Again she wondered where Grandy's oldest offspring was, why he hadn't been at the hospital, and why no one there had mentioned his absence.

When anyone asked her what had happened that afternoon, Amber told all she knew about Grandy's condition. She didn't tell anyone else about the charade she and Bradley enacted, and she knew she could trust Zita to keep the story to herself. To Amber it seemed that telling what they'd had to do would make Grandy an object of pity—a frail, old woman to be patronized and deceived in her final hours. Besides, it was no one else's business.

By eight-thirty the building had cleared, but an emergency board meeting had been called for Saturday afternoon. At ten-thirty, Spencer Bailey called from the hospital and asked Zita to reserve the entire next day to work for the board members. That would leave Tam and Amber alone in the center, but the weekends were usually quiet this time of year.

At about eleven Amber went up to Bradley's office. She'd never actually seen it because she'd been saving that for a special moment. But after what had happened earlier, she'd decided to leave him a note asking about Grandy and offering to help if there was anything else she could do. She was certain Bradley would know her offer was sincere. As soon as she rounded the corner she saw the strip of light under the door and her heart began to thump. He was in there. Alone.

The door was slightly ajar, and rather than knock Amber pushed it open. Bradley sat forward in his chair, his elbows propped on the desk and his fingers tangled in his thick hair. His broad shoulders strained against his white cotton shirt, and even sitting there motionless and obviously fatigued, an aura of masculine vitality still clung to him. Because he was so still, Amber wondered if he'd been overcome by exhaustion and fallen asleep with his head in his hands. Then the door creaked slightly, and he looked up.

When he saw who it was he smiled, and the pleasure on his face curled through Amber like a sweet note of music.

"Well," he said wearily, "if it isn't my angel. I was just thinking about you."

Amber felt herself blushing and was glad the lights at her end of the room were dim. "I was going to leave you a note." She lifted her hand to show it to him. "How is she?"

He took a heavy breath. "I don't know. The same I guess. One minute she seems fine and the next minute she's delirious. They're talking stroke."

"Oh, no."

He pinched the bridge of his nose and squeezed his eyelids shut. "Well, nothing's for sure yet. They're still doing tests."

Amber heard the disgust in his tone. She knew exactly how he was feeling. During Daddo's illness she had become intimately familiar with vague diagnoses, noncommittal analyses and the endlessly frustrating processes of hospitals and doctors. "I know this isn't much help, but I'm sure they're doing all they can."

Bradley gave her a doubtful glance. "Yeah, I'll just bet they are."

"Really, I know how crazy it makes you feel when no one can tell you anything definite, but Burdyne is a good hospital. I'm sure she's getting the best care available."

The corner of his mouth gave a sardonic little twist. "That's exactly what I'm afraid of."

Amber could see the exhaustion and worry etched into every aspect of his body—his skin looked gray and his eyes were bloodshot. The muscular shoulders almost sagged with fatigue, but papers were strewn on his desk as if he were in the middle of a workday. How long had he been up? she wondered. She vaguely remembered him saying something about having to drive in from somewhere. Was it the ranch?

"Have you had anything to eat?" she asked.

"No. Well, not any real food. Somebody bought muffins out of a machine, but they tasted like a mixture of sawdust and spackling compound."

Amber nodded. She had ingested that particular treat a time or two. "If you like, I could go get you something. Since it's this late, it'll have to be tacos or a burger or something, but there're a couple of places open all night long down Westheimer."

He shook his head. "Thanks, but I don't think I could eat anything like that. But would you—" He hesitated, then his mouth closed. Obviously, he'd decided not to finish his question.

"What?"

He looked up at her. "Would you consider going with me to get something? La Jaliscience is open until four, and the Spanish Flower is open all night long. Or we could go get breakfast. I just don't want to . . . eat alone."

He's inviting me out to dinner? Amber feared her mouth was gaping open fishlike and that her eyes were bugging out of her head. "Is it all right for me to leave? I mean, I don't think I'm supposed to leave the building during my shift."

Bradley dropped his head to one side. "Well, for the time being at least, I'm still a vice president of this company. If Mrs. Fugate or anyone else in Accounting questions your time card, send her to me."

"In that case, I accept."

"Uh, one more thing..."

Amber grinned. "I'm driving?"

He smiled sheepishly. "Right."

He slipped his coat on, and they walked together through the darkened atrium, past the pools of lights haloing the Egyptian art on pedestals and the Impressionist paintings of water lilies and beautiful women wearing garden hats and gauzy dresses. Amber told herself to remember this moment, to etch it into whatever nook or cranny of memory held the moments of sweetest significance. She had a feeling they were moving in one of those islands of time that occurs in the midst of upheavals or tragedies. They would make pleasant conversation over a late dinner, maybe share childhood stories or favorite movies while a storm brewed around them that would break at any moment.

They rode in silence down the elevator, and when Amber peeked around the corner of the night staff office to tell the others where she was going, Zita gave her a huge smile and a thumbs-up. Tam gawked.

Their footsteps echoed in the empty garage, and Bradley took Amber's keys and unlocked the door for her. She felt a sudden wave of embarrassment at the clutter in her pickup. Earlier—when Bradley had been frantic to get to the hospital by any means available—it didn't matter, but now she wished fervently that she was one of those people who were relentlessly neat and tidy.

In Amber's truck, however, cassette tapes, schoolbooks and old papers nested in crumpled piles on the floorboard and the passenger seat. A heavy, red antitheft device she hadn't used in months poked out from beneath a floor mat, and the metallic rattle of aluminum cans revealed the fact that she didn't always recycle in a timely fashion.

Amber raked at the books and papers. "Please excuse the mess. I've been at the beach and I haven't had a chance to—"

"This is nothing," Bradley lied gallantly. "You should see my car."

Amber knew he was being solicitous. She had seen his car. In fact, she'd practically smashed her nose against the squeaky clean windshield every time she'd passed it parked in the garage. The only clutter she'd ever noticed in the Italian convertible was an occasional squash racquet or gym bag.

He chuckled. "Anyway, at least yours runs."

Amber laughed, too. "So, you've been having some car trouble?"

He shook his head in disgust. "Lately, it happens all the time. I've spent a fortune on tune-ups and parts and expert opinions, but every now and then, it just quits. Drives me nuts. It seems to happen whenever I'm really in a hurry to get somewhere. Damned thing."

Amber made a sympathetic noise. "Maybe that's just when you notice it the most. Why don't you get rid of it?"

He shrugged. "I should, I suppose, but I'm afraid it's become a matter of principle."

Amber peered at him through her eyelashes. "A matter of principle? I'm sorry, but this sounds like a stubborn, guy thing to me."

"Maybe. I suppose we're locked in a battle of wills."

"'Scuse me, but isn't one of you a car?"

He grinned again. "Like you said, it's a guy thing. You female types wouldn't understand."

Amber started the truck and drove up the exit ramp. As soon as the front wheels hit the pressure plate, the metal security gate rolled up and the two of them drove out of the parking lot and into the soft, navy night. Amber was acutely aware of the man beside her, his size, the remnants of after-shave and whatever it was he washed his hair with, the way his pant legs pulled against his strong thighs.

They decided it was too late for Mexican food and instead drove to Harlow's, a Hollywood-style after-hours place on the corner of Hillcroft and Richmond. An enormous black-and-white portrait of Jean Harlow dominated the art deco dining room, and Tiffany lamps hung low over every booth. The walls were painted a dark forest green, but were almost completely obscured by scores of photographs of movie stars from the Golden Age of Hollywood.

An extremely thin young man in a vintage tuxedo escorted them to one of the booths, and Amber slid into her side. She was glad she'd worn a dress to work; the appreciatively assessing looks of the waiters boosted her confidence. Earlier that day she'd thought she looked her best, but a little confirmation went a long way. Especially if you suddenly find yourself out with the man of your dreams. Or at least, the object of your desire.

Bradley waited until Amber was seated to take his place, then he ordered a carafe of coffee. He asked Amber if she preferred something else.

"Coffee's fine," she said. Her nerves were screaming for a Margarita, but she did have to go back to work and Bradley was, after all, the boss.

As soon as he dropped into his place opposite her, Amber's worst fears materialized. Silence settled over them like an airless tent. Her nose itched, and she thought she could hear her watch ticking. Although she wasn't the least bit thirsty, she took a drink of water. Then inspiration struck.

"What are you going to do about the car? I mean, will a wrecker have to come and get it?"

Disgust flickered across his face, and Amber's heart sank. *That's right, bring up a sore subject.*

"I guess. Once again, Rudy's Roadsters gets to gouge me. I think I'm sending his son through law school."

Amber chuckled. "Well, tuition is high."

Their waiter appeared with heavy mugs and a carafe of steaming coffee. Harlow's was famous for its three-egg omelettes, and Amber ordered hers with mushrooms and cheese. Bradley ordered the Western omelette special with bell peppers, onions and sausage topped with hot ranchero sauce. All the breakfasts came with sides of cottage fries and piles of Texas toast. The waiter filled their mugs, took their order and disappeared.

That was the moment when Amber caught Bradley looking at her bare shoulders. His mouth had opened slightly and Amber knew—the way a woman always knows—that he was feeling desire for her. Maybe he was just tired and discouraged and needing comfort. Or maybe it was because she felt beautiful in his presence, and somehow that information had communicated itself to him. At that moment the reason didn't matter. Just knowing that he wanted her filled Amber with feminine confidence. She smiled her sweetest and most inviting smile at him, and saw it thud into him like one of Cupid's arrows.

Bradley's eyes connected with hers, and Amber's breath stopped. He cleared his throat. "Were those—did I see schoolbooks in your truck?"

"Yes. As a matter of fact, you did. I'm taking twelve hours this semester at the Central Campus."

"Twelve hours. That's a lot. Where? Rice or Houston Baptist—"

Amber laughed a little. "Oh, no. Neither. University of Houston. I could never afford a private school. And besides, I never made the grades to get into a school like Rice."

"What's your degree plan?"

Amber felt a clutch to her middle. He was treading on very sensitive ground, and she was never sure she wanted to share this with anyone. What if she told him and he reacted like some of the others? She'd stopped telling people the truth a long time ago because she couldn't bear the glazed looks they gave her. The condescension. This was the central issue of her life, and if Bradley Ackerman—the man of her dreams—sneered, well, she'd probably dissolve into tears.

It was now or never. She bucked up her courage and took a deep breath. "Education."

"Really?" He straightened up slightly. "You want to be a teacher?"

Her spine was still rigid with wariness. She hoped it didn't show on her face. "That's right."

"What level?"

Another silent breath, the clenching of muscles. "Elementary."

"So you want to work with little kids."

She smiled inwardly. He seemed interested if not exactly overwhelmed. "Yeah, I do."

"Is somebody in your family a teacher?"

"No. Just me."

"Hmm." He nodded and took a sip of coffee. "How much longer until you graduate?"

Her heart sank. This was the worst part. She was, after all, twenty-seven years old. "At least two more years."

"Oh," he said nodding. "I guess it's hard working full-time and going to school, too."

"Yes," she said. "It is."

"What made you choose elementary ed?"

She'd never told anyone outside her family this story. Actually, no one had ever asked. Usually when she said she wanted to be a teacher, people made patronizing "How nice" noises and then began to pick lint off their clothes. Something about the way Bradley looked at her told her he was genuinely interested. She knew he didn't realize what he was asking her to share with him; to him it was probably just a polite and casual question.

Well, she told herself, time to see what your fantasy man is made of. If he understands, maybe he really is the one; but if he starts looking bored, you'll know he's not.

"It's kind of a long story."

"I'd like to hear it," he said.

Amber heard the weariness in his voice. He'd had a horrible day and was under grinding pressure. Maybe he was just grateful for any quiet distraction.

"I always loved school. I have two sisters, Scarlet and Vi. Vi's brilliant. If she reads something once or twice it's committed to memory, but Scarlet's a true genius. She never had to study at all."

"Two sisters?" Bradley interrupted.

"Right."

"No brothers?"

"No brothers." Amber looked down. "I have kind of an unusual family. My sisters are half sisters. My mom married Vi's dad when she was seventeen. They divorced before she was twenty. Then she married my dad, and he was killed in a construction accident before she even knew she was pregnant with me."

"You never met your dad?"

"No." As a matter of fact, Amber only had one photograph of him—a blond, hazel-eyed man with her face, wearing tacky, striped bell-bottoms, a poet's shirt and an enormous grin. A stiff wind blew the long, curly hair away from his face, and his arms were wrapped around Amber's mother as they stood on the upstairs deck of the Balinese Room in Galveston. Maude's face was radiant with joy, and her waist-length black hair hung in a dark curtain over her shoulders.

Amber shrugged. "They say I'm just like him—that I have his disposition. Isn't it strange we never even met?"

"Sometimes a person's nature is a matter of heredity."

For a moment Amber thought she saw sadness flash through Bradley's eyes, but he busied himself pouring and stirring sugar into his coffee, so she went on with her story.

"His name was Harold. Isn't that awful? But his nickname was Hap, short for Happy."

Bradley looked up and smiled. "Now, that doesn't surprise me. You seem happy."

"Well," Amber said, "I am."

There was a moment of thoughtful silence.

"You were talking about school."

"Oh, yeah. Anyway, I wasn't nearly as smart as Scarlet or Vi, but I was involved in a lot of activities all through high school. You know, sports, student council, clubs—all that sort of thing."

"Cheerleading, too, I bet."

Amber laughed a little and shrugged. "It seems embarrassing now, but, yeah, that, too."

Bradley shook his head and the twinkle appeared in his eye. "Nothing to be embarrassed about. I've always liked cheerleaders."

"Anyway," Amber said, "I had to work really hard for my grades. But I liked school. I liked it so much, and I was interested in so many things that for the first three years, I kept changing my major. History, literature, fine arts." She wrinkled her nose. "I even tried the School of Business once. Ugh. Economics, what a nightmare."

"They say liberal arts is the only real education," Bradley offered generously.

"Thank you for saying that. Even if it's not true, I appreciate it. My parents finally got disgusted with me since they were paying for everything. I mean, my grades were good, but it didn't look like I was ever going to graduate. So about five years ago they suggested that I take a year off to think and travel. Daddo, my stepdad—he's Scarlet's father—anyway Daddo's business was doing great and I knew plenty of people in Europe—"

"Really?"

"Yeah, we were an American Field Service family so we had foreign kids in our house for years. Anyway, there was always the Youth Hostel Association, and I had lots of families to stay with, so the plan was for me to spend three months each in four different countries. I left in May and spent the summer in Ibiza. My friend Teresa and I went all over Spain and Portugal. Then in September I went to Cambridge."

"England's great. I wish I'd spent more time there."

"Me, too. Anyway, in October I was taking a bus from Bath up to Edinburgh and there was a freak ice storm in

York. Two or three buses had to stop at one of those awful roadside bus stop places."

Brad scowled. "Seen 'em. Dismal."

"To say the least. Anyway, there must have been forty people stuck there, couples, kids, old people. After about ten hours we were getting to know each other pretty well, and some of us were taking turns entertaining the kids. You know, reading to them and all."

Amber stopped. This was the hard part. "There was one little girl, Meg. I guess she was about seven. Anyway, she seemed really desperate for attention. She sat right by me. There were about ten of us in a circle passing picture books around and taking turns reading and letting the kids read. When the book came to me, I put my arm around her, and I asked her if she wanted to read aloud. But she—" The memory still seared, even after all this time, and Amber had to stop for a moment.

She cleared her throat. "At first she just sat there, and I could feel her beginning to shake. Then she put her face in her hands and started crying. 'I can't,' she said. I said, 'Yes, you can. Don't be shy.' And she looked up at me, and she had these huge brown eyes just streaming tears. No, miss,' she said. 'I can't read.'"

Amber sighed. "Well, you can imagine how I felt. The other children started laughing and telling her she was thick, which is English slang for—"

"Stupid," Bradley said with disgust. "I know."

"God," Amber said, "I felt horrible. At first I couldn't imagine how she'd gotten so big without learning to read. Then I saw her mother. She was my age or maybe a little younger, twenty-two—maybe twenty-three. Besides Meg she had a little boy about four and a toddler, and she was holding an infant in her lap. She looked absolutely demented with exhaustion. She said she was trying to join her husband in Liverpool where he'd finally gotten a job. Apparently the family moved around a lot, and the children never got settled into school.

"Anyway, I found Meg and got her mopped up and calmed down, and then I took her off to a corner, and the two of us started drawing pictures. It turned out that she knew the alphabet, but she didn't know phonics, so I drew pictures like mouse for *M,* egg for *E,* goat for *G.*

"In less than thirty minutes, I wrote her name and she sounded it out. She said 'Meg.' Then she looked up at me and back down at the paper. 'That's my name,' she said, and her eyes got huge. For a minute she sat still as a rock, and then she shot straight up in the chair and grabbed the paper off the table. It was like somebody turned a light on inside her. She started shouting, 'I can read.' Then she ran all the way through this dingy bus stop café shouting, 'Mama, I can read.'"

Amber had to stop for a moment; the memory still choked her up. "I can't tell you how that made me feel. I realized that was the only important thing I'd ever done in my life."

"And that's when you decided—"

"To be a teacher. I'd never been so certain about anything in my life." *Well, there was one other thing....*

Bradley's brows creased, "But that was five years ago, you said. You didn't go back to school right away? Didn't your parents approve of your decision?"

Amber turned her coffee cup in her hands. "When my bus got to Edinburgh, there was a message waiting for me. Daddo was terribly sick, in the hospital and not expected to live. I had to get on a plane and come right back."

She sighed. "He was very sick for a very long time. He had to retire and sell the business, and money got really tight. You know, even when you think you have enough insurance, it costs a fortune to stay in the hospital—especially for months. Anyway, there was no way they could afford to support me and send me to school like before. Besides, I just couldn't have taken money from them. So I had to start working full time and take classes whenever I could."

"That's a pretty cruel irony, isn't it? The minute you realize what you want to do with your life, all these obstacles appear."

"Well, I tell myself everything happens for a reason. Maybe the forces of the universe just want to test my resolve. But nothing," she said quietly, "nothing will stop me from doing this. I don't care if it takes ten years. I'm going to be a teacher. I'm going to teach children how to read."

Bradley didn't reply aloud to what she said, but Amber saw something new in his expression when he looked at her. She couldn't decide if it was admiration or if he'd decided she was completely nuts.

Chapter Five

At that moment their waiter appeared balancing a tray, which he swung around in front of them with a flourish. "I have a Western here with ranchero." Bradley leaned back, and the artfully garnished platter was set in front of him. "And one mushroom-onion-cheese."

The omelettes were steaming and framed with sizzling cottage fries. Melted cheese, mushrooms and sautéed vegetables spilled out onto the enormous white plates and, before disappearing, the waiter set down a teetering stack of Texas toast and a scoop of pale butter in an iced dish.

Bradley watched surreptitiously as Amber shook salt and pepper and a liberal dose of hot sauce over her omelette. When the shining curtain of her hair swung forward, she unconsciously pushed it behind her ear. So pretty, he thought. So unpretentious.

Amber Oakland was nothing like the women he usually went out with. Not that the two of them were going out. This was more like taking his secretary to lunch. He thought of Mrs. Lukenbach, her trifocals, sturdy shoes and sausagelike arms.

Actually, this was nothing like taking his secretary out to lunch.

He took a hefty swig of scalding coffee and tried not to stare at Amber's tanned shoulders. *What's wrong with you? She's a nice person. Think of what she's put up with today.* Tovah would never have done it. Or if she had, she would have exacted her pound of flesh in return.

Bradley understood Tovah, her motives and her outlook on life. Women like Tovah were demanding and impatient. They didn't have relationships, they cut deals. Bradley was comfortable with that. He had been for years. Better to have tacit understandings than the unpredictability of "relationships." There would be no hurt feelings, no unmet expectations, no heartbreaking betrayals.

Why are you even thinking this way? You're just having breakfast with the woman. He glanced up and caught a glimpse of the smattering of freckles across the bridge of Amber's nose, the shining, scrubbed complexion and full lower lip. He'd kissed that mouth earlier that day. At that memory, he felt a familiar stirring. He reached for the ice water.

"How's your omelette?" Amber asked.

"Just great."

She frowned slightly when she looked down at his plate and saw that it was untouched.

He grinned. "I mean, I'm sure it's great. I eat here a lot."

She nodded, and her loose hair swung around her shoulders.

Face it, buddy, sneered a sarcastic inner voice—a voice of grating familiarity—*you want to take her home.* He looked away. Of course he wanted to take her home. Who wouldn't? She was beautiful in a perky, hometown girl way, and she was sweet. She had a nice smile and those big hazel eyes.

Those aren't her eyes you're staring at. The tantalizing swell of breasts softened the angles of her collarbones, and Bradley did his best to force his gaze elsewhere. But everything about her was gentle and inviting. And pleasing. She was the kind of woman you could cuddle up with on a sofa in front of a fire.

He thought of Tovah and her elegant emaciation. Making love to Tovah would be like throwing himself naked on coat hangers. Amber seemed to be all tanned skin and inviting curves and sunshine.

Just the kind of woman an Ackerman would avoid if he had any conscience at all, he told himself. She's been nothing but nice to you. Leave her alone. As a matter of fact, the smartest and nicest thing you could do would be to put this situation back on an employer-employee basis.

"What made you decide to go to work at the company?"

Amber set her fork down. "Well, for one thing, the hours. Since I'm off during the day, I can go to school."

"Didn't you ever work at night before?"

Her mouth puckered in a pretty grimace. "Yeah. I tried waitressing, but the money wasn't great and the work was exhausting. I didn't have any energy left over for school. Actually, I almost flunked out. I thought about working the late shift in a convenience store—"

"That's too dangerous."

"I know. The thought of it terrified my folks, and they made me promise I wouldn't do it." She tore a corner of toast away, and Bradley noticed her hands, the short, rounded nails and lack of polish or silk wraps or whatever the hell it was that the women in his crowd used to make their fingernails look like talons. Hands like Amber's worked in flower beds, smoothed medicine over scraped knees and held storybooks.

"That's why I jumped at the chance to work at your... the company. The job's a lifesaver for me. I'm finally making real progress toward my degree. As a matter of fact, it's the best job I've ever had." She looked up at him with earnest golden eyes. "I can't say enough about what working at the company means to me. Because of this job, my dreams are coming true."

Bradley shifted uncomfortably. "Well, I'm sure you're really qualified or you wouldn't have been hired."

A huge, sunshiny smile broke across her face. "Yeah, I guess so."

She picked up her napkin and dabbed the corner of her mouth. Bradley liked the way she moved. Her arms were firm and had a pleasingly taut curve without hard, bony edges. She looked athletic—maybe tennis, he thought, or racquetball. Not weights, though. She just didn't seem like the type to spend hours at the gym scrutinizing every curve and angle of her flesh in mirrored, wraparound walls.

He decided Amber Oakland looked exactly like what she was—a pretty, unspoiled, unpretentious girl who was going to be a wonderful teacher, and who would someday make some nice guy a perfect wife. From that point on, he was determined to keep the conversation casual, no more personal stuff—just a little company history. Definitely nothing about himself.

Earlier he was pretty sure he detected a glimmer of interest in the way she spoke and looked at him. Nothing as blatant as flirting, but he didn't want to take a chance that she might become attracted to him. After all, he might not be able to do the right thing.

He remembered the way her eyes teared up when she spoke with Grandy, all the sweetness and comfort she offered him in that one kiss. And what about the story about Meg, and how that had convinced her to teach children to read? She was a sweetheart. Then he thought of her tanned and taut little body, and his own body responded to the memory. He spread his napkin carefully across his lap. No, he couldn't be expected to resist that. What man could?

Especially if he was an Ackerman.

From that point on he steered their conversation toward neutral, innocuous subjects. When the waiter passed by them again, he asked for the check, paid cash and left a generous tip.

As they walked to her truck, he offered to drive, and though she looked surprised, she accepted. They talked cars during the short drive, and once back at the office, he thanked her one more time, said a brisk good-night and then went straight up to his office.

In less than an hour he'd cleaned off his desk and called a cab to take him home. This, he promised himself, was the first, last and only time he would ever spend time alone with the pretty woman who'd been sitting opposite him. He still had that much restraint and compassion. And decency.

Maybe they worked in the same building, but he would simply arrange his schedule so that he never saw her again.

"I'm sure he wants to see me again," Amber said to Violet. They'd been on the phone for more than half an hour, while Amber related every detail she could remember of the day before.

"What makes you so sure?"

"I just know. The way he looked at me. The sweet things he said. I could tell he was attracted to me."

"Being attracted is one thing, asking you out is another."

Amber made a exasperated sound. "Why are you being negative?"

"I just don't want you to get hurt."

Amber didn't argue with her oldest sister. Violet had spent years perfecting the art of not getting hurt. Amber didn't blame her, either. Vi's father had made it clear from the start that he wanted nothing to do with his daughter. The rest of the Fortescue family shunned her, as well, because they despised Maude for deliberately getting pregnant to trap their only son into a teenage marriage. Amber had often wondered if Louis Fortescue's participation in the precipitating event was ever considered.

Amber also knew that years ago—when Violet was sixteen—she made a surprise trip to finally meet her father face-to-face. After she came back she never mentioned him again, and all the old photographs of him she'd kept like a shrine in her bedroom disappeared forever.

After graduation from the University of Texas, Violet came back to Galveston where she worked as a librarian. Over the years she'd fashioned herself what seemed to be a serene life—her music, the museums, her cats and her books. Although Amber often wondered if more went on under that calm surface than any of them suspected, Vi never hinted at any mad passions, and no one asked.

Despite their different personalities, Amber confided in Vi more often than Scarlet or her mother. Maude had too many worries, and Scarlet's formidable temper made her a prickly and volatile choice of confidante. Although Amber often thought Vi was overly cautious, she also thought her older sister made up for what she lacked in imagination with plain good sense.

"But I'm not going to get hurt, Vi. He's the one. I'm sure of it."

"Please be careful."

"I will. You know me."

"Yes," she said. "I do."

"Well, listen, sweetie," Amber said, "the work's really stacked up so I better go. Love ya."

"I love you, too."

Amber had never experienced a weekend this busy at Ackerman. When she'd pulled into the parking lot earlier that day, the first thing she noticed was the extra fifteen or so cars parked close to the door. The hallways were silent, but the tension and waiting atmosphere hung in the building as thick and palpable as a heavy fog. When she walked into the center, she was greeted by the sight of an overflowing In basket and a stack of telecopies to be sent. Despite the news that Grandy was holding her own at the hospital, the board was obviously preparing for the worst.

Since Zita had been drafted to work on the sixth floor with the board members, Amber worked alone in the center for the first part of the day. Amber didn't envy her friend. Even sitting five floors away from the board meeting, all day long, haggard, curt-speaking men she didn't recognize brought her a steady stream of documents for revision. She could hardly imagine the kind of day Zita must be having.

At about three Amber thought she heard someone coming down the hall and turned toward the door just as a hatchet-faced, stony-eyed man entered, carrying a sheaf of papers and an alligator skin portfolio. He dropped the briefcase on the desk, missing her hands only because she whipped them away. He had a high forehead, thinning reddish-blond hair and cold green eyes. "I need this revised and printed out in triple space."

"Right. Shall I phone you when I'm done?"

"Yes."

Amber glanced through the heavily marked draft. "What's your extension, please?"

"Just leave a message on my voice mail. You'll find the number in the directory...if that's not too challenging for you." He strode out without waiting for Amber to reply. She stared after him for one thunderstruck moment.

"Well, thank you, Mr. Charm."

Amber had never seen the man before and had no idea how to look up his number. She shook her head, sighed and went to work. Later on when Zita came back, Amber would describe the jerk to her. Zita would know who he was.

At about five that afternoon, Zita returned—her face red and her eyes glistening with anger.

"What's wrong?"

"That damned Phillip Ackerman," she said. "Nobody'll work for him because he's so nasty, but I didn't have a choice, since I was the only secretary up there."

"What happened?"

She gave an angry flap of her hand. "Oh, it's not worth mentioning. Just typical behavior from him. But he likes to wait until you're in a group of people and then make snotty remarks. He asked me to get coffee for them, and when I turned around he said I looked like..." She took a deep breath. "Oh, it's not worth mentioning. At least he keeps his big mouth shut when Mr. Bailey's around."

"Is Mr. Bailey still up there?"

Amber thought she might go up and ask how Grandy was doing.

"No. He just went back to the hospital." She leaned forward and lowered her voice. "Apparently Mrs. Ackerman wants to change a bunch of stuff in her will, and there's some shuffling around of family property going on. The company's not the only thing that's going to go through some changes."

"How can she do that if she's so sick?"

Zita shrugged. "Beats me. I didn't have time to read whatever it was. I had to type with Mr. Bailey standing over me watching every sentence. It makes me nuts when somebody looks over my shoulder when I'm trying to type."

Amber murmured sympathetically and tried to keep her tone casual. "By the way, is Bradley up there?"

Zita nodded. "They're all up there shouting their heads off at each other—the family, the board members. I don't know what's going on, but something's happening."

"Some guy came in here earlier. He left this for me to revise. I'm supposed to call him when I'm done, but he didn't tell me his name."

Amber described the man. His height, hair and attitude.

Zita sighed. "Guess who?"

"That was Bradley's dad?"

Zita nodded and muttered an anatomical epithet.

They divided the remaining work, and Amber took her stack back to her own cubicle. Things quieted down by seven, and Zita left early, totally shattered from her day. Amber had thought Bradley might come by to tell her how Grandy was, but he didn't. By midnight she knew he wasn't going to call her. She told herself he was just exhausted and preoccupied with his own crushing burdens. She also knew she didn't have a right to expect him to keep her informed, but something inside her felt wistful. And left out.

On Sunday the office was quiet in a spooky, watchful way. The boardroom remained empty as did all the executive offices. Zita sat at the front desk, reading the Sunday paper, and Amber opened her books and tried valiantly to compose meaningful sentences about the Dingley Tariff of 1897, but she simply couldn't concentrate.

Finally she gave up, and at four o'clock she phoned the hospital.

"Burdyne Memorial."

"ICU, please."

"Just a moment."

Amber was put on hold, and syrupy, canned music flowed through the earpiece.

"ICU."

"Hello, this is Amber Oakland at Ackerman Drilling. I'm phoning to see if Estelle Ackerman, the chairman, has been moved to a room yet. We want to send flowers."

"Just a minute."

Left on hold for the second time, Amber tried to remain patient while once again the violins sawed away.

"Who were you holding for?"

"Um, we were phoning to see if Mrs. Ackerman has been moved to a room—"

"She's gone."

"What?"

"I just came on, and she's not here. She was in One-A and it's been cleaned."

"Has she been sent to a room?"

A disgusted sigh preceded another interlude of insipid elevator sounds. Amber began to feel twinges of alarm. What did she mean? *Gone.*

Dread wormed its way through her conscious. None of the family had been to the office all day. Not one of the board members had even phoned. Surely Grandy wasn't...

"Hello."

"Yes, I was on hold. I'm trying to find out where Mrs. Ackerman has been moved."

"She's not registered."

"But she was in ICU last night. Did something happen to her?"

"Are you family?"

"No, I'm an employee at Ackerman Drill—"

"Well, I'm afraid we're not allowed to give information to anyone other than the family. Sorry."

Click. Buzz.

"Oh, no."

Zita appeared at the corner. "What's wrong?"

"That was the hospital. They said Grandy's gone."

"Gone where?"

"They wouldn't tell me anything because I'm not family."

"Did she check out?"

"They wouldn't say."

"You don't think . . ."

Amber swallowed. "I don't know. We could call someone at home, I suppose. Bradley or maybe Mr. Bailey."

Zita had emergency night numbers for all the members of the board. There was no answer at Bradley's apartment or at Phillip Ackerman's house. When Amber got a recording at Spencer Bailey's town house she began to lose heart.

"Maybe we shouldn't do this."

Zita bit her lip. "Maybe not. I suppose, I mean, if something *has* happened somebody'll call us."

No one had to call Amber. She had a gut feeling that something awful was about to happen. Prayers were even beyond her. She merely sat at her station, her mind vacillating anxiously from one unhappy scenario to another.

She wished she could be with Bradley to offer him sympathy and an understanding shoulder. But, after all, she wasn't his girlfriend.

She sat in her chair and let her head fall into her hands. Why do I feel so sad? she wondered. I only met her one time. Why do I feel like I've lost somebody I love?

Amber remembered Grandy's soft, powdered cheek and her dignity and strength despite the invasion of tubes and monitors and needles. She remembered the love and sadness shining out of old but brilliantly blue eyes. *Kiss her for me, Bradley... you'll be doing it in front of a church full of people, but I won't be there.*

Amber heard footsteps entering the office and dropped her face onto her arms. Zita would handle it. Even with her head down, though, Amber was suddenly aware that someone now stood beside her cubicle.

"Amber?"

She looked up. "Bradley."

Pain had carved itself into every plane and angle of his handsome face. Usually so impeccably dressed, he wore faded blue jeans and a white shirt that appeared to have been slept in; he hadn't shaved. His eyes were the worst, though, so filled with sadness and regret. Amber's breath caught. Something had sent him to her in this terrible time. He stood close—barely two feet away—and yet he seemed unable to reach out to her across the tiny space that separated them. She rose.

"I called the hospital," she said softly.

She saw her words slice into him, opening his wounds. He pinched his eyes shut. "I wanted to tell you first."

From the corner of her eye, Amber saw Zita slip discreetly out the door. The flickering of lights on the phone set told her that all the lines had been forwarded into hold.

Wonderful Zita, Amber thought, to take care of every little thing.

"They told me she was gone...but no details. They wouldn't say anything since I'm not family." She took another step nearer. The pain and exhaustion radiating from him made her ache to hold him and offer whatever comfort she had to give.

He nodded. "Then no one else has called you, either?"

She shook her head. "No."

"Well," he said, dragging a weary hand over his eyes, "I suppose that's because they don't know you work on the night staff. Spencer does, but of course he wouldn't say anything."

Amber didn't quite understand what he was implying. Why would anyone in Bradley's family want to call her? And what did Spencer Bailey know that the others might want to find out about her? She thought Bradley might be disoriented. She knew that terrible grief, coupled with extreme fatigue, sometimes did that to people. And Bradley was obviously suffering from both.

She couldn't bear seeing his pain unconsoled for another minute. Taking a deep breath, she closed the distance between them and put her arms around him.

"I'm so sorry," she said. "I wish I'd gotten to know her better. She was an extraordinary woman."

She rested her head against his chest, and his heart thudded away right by her cheek. She felt the warm, solid muscle of his back beneath her hands, the deep groove where his spine nested. For a moment he hesitated to hold her, obviously overwhelmed by her embrace, but Amber didn't mind.

He needed her, she was there.

He cleared his throat, and his hands rested lightly on her shoulders. Hesitation kept his arms tentative even as they closed around her. "Amber?"

"Mmm?"

"What are you talking about?"

She looked up, knowing her eyes were glassy with tears. "Your grandmother. I wish I'd gotten to know her before she . . . before it was too late."

He blinked. His eyes cut to the left, then closed. "You don't know," he muttered.

Amber leaned back slightly to get a better view of his face. He took her upper arms firmly in his hands. "You'd better sit down."

Something gleefully ominous danced across Amber's stomach. She pulled her chair out, and Bradley sat on the corner of her desk.

"The hospital—when they told you Grandy was gone—they didn't mean she passed away, they meant she left."

"What?"

He nodded. "Apparently she woke up feeling . . . invigorated this morning and asked for a hot breakfast. They brought her oatmeal, which, uh, disappointed her, and she threw it on her doctor."

Amber couldn't control the extremely unladylike snort of laughter which erupted from her throat. "But that's wonderful news. They discharged her then? So quickly?" Amber knew her eyes had grown huge. "They didn't throw her out or anything, just for that?"

For some reason Bradley wouldn't look at her directly. "No, they didn't throw her out. Actually, she got her purse and an extra hospital gown." He cleared his throat. "One to cover up her, uh, backside, and then she called Harris, her driver. Then she walked out."

"You're kidding."

"No. I'm not."

"What does her doctor say?"

"He says we owe him four hundred dollars for a new pair of frames." He shrugged and glanced up at her. "She hit him on the nose with the oatmeal, and his glasses flew off."

Amber chuckled again. "She's really something."

"Yeah. She always has been."

"You don't look very happy?"

"Well, that's not all."

He appeared to be struggling to gather his thoughts, and Amber sat quietly. He must be worried sick about Grandy's condition, she thought. Then a new thought struck her—wasn't it wonderful of him to come all the way to the office to tell her in person? Obviously he was beginning to care for her. She knew she'd been right about the blossoming attraction she'd sensed at the restaurant. Well, this was definite confirmation.

"Did you know that my whole family gathered?"

Amber nodded. "Yes, except your sister in Dallas."

"Right. Suzette's baby is due pretty soon—her first—and she's been having some trouble. And the entire board flew in for the meeting yesterday."

"I know. We were really busy all day."

"Well, since everyone was here, and she was feeling so recovered, Grandy decided it was a perfect time to have a party."

"A party? Is she up to it?"

Bradley shrugged. "That doesn't matter. It's going to happen one way or the other. Tomorrow night."

Suspicion finally dawned in the silence that ensued. Amber narrowed her eyes. Bradley didn't look up.

"What kind of party?"

He winced, and finally his eyes met hers. "An engagement party."

Chapter Six

Amber's stomach lurched, and she felt a slickness on her palms. "You're kidding."

He shook his head. "I wish I were."

"But... but what—"

"Would you come upstairs for a few minutes? Spencer's waiting in his office, and I think we should all talk."

Amber stood and followed him. She knew she was moving like a marionette. What did this mean? What would the family say when they told them the truth? What would Grandy say?

Amber swallowed. Would she lose her job? Surely Bradley wouldn't let that happen. If he could help it.

Her mind tumbled. They'd only been trying to make a dying woman happy. How did that turn into this huge complicated crisis? Well, maybe she was borrowing trouble. Maybe it would all work out just fine, and they could all go back to the way things were before.

Yes, she decided, just some good, honest revelation—embarrassing for them maybe—but then everything would be just as it was before.

They passed Zita in the hallway.

"Zita," Bradley said firmly, "if anyone calls asking where Amber is, would you tell them she left with me?"

"S-sure."

"If it's an emergency, we'll be in Mr. Bailey's office, but don't tell anyone that. Call me first. And if anyone from my family just shows up, please tell them you don't know where we went. Okay?"

She nodded, her eyes as round as moons.

The silent ride up the elevator did nothing to calm Amber's nerves. She stole little glances at Bradley out of the corner of her eye. Tension tightened the angles of his face, but this was different from when they'd been racing to the hospital. He wasn't frantic in the least, but there was definitely something else. Fear niggled through her thoughts. He was dreading the conversation they were about to have. Bradley obviously thought something really bad was going to happen.

Amber also had the distinct impression he wasn't afraid for himself.

She swallowed again. If not himself, then whom?

Spencer Bailey stood staring out his window with his hands clasped behind his back. He wore a dark, pin-striped suit, and gold glimmered at the cuffs of his crisp white shirt; his back was parade-ground straight.

Dressed for battle, Amber thought.

When he turned around, his expression was very grave. "Amber," he said. "Thank you for coming."

"Of course, Mr. Bailey."

"Please," he said. "Call me Spencer. I suppose Bradley has told you what's happening?"

She nodded. "Yes, he did. I'm so glad Gr—Mrs. Ackerman's feeling better. Do the doctors have any idea what happened? Is her heart okay?"

Bradley pulled a chair out for her. "The tests all came back inconclusive." He took the seat beside her. "If you can believe them," he added darkly. "We finally found her doctor. He didn't tell us he'd gone fishing in Mexico. I intend to discuss that with him. Soon."

Bailey took the seat behind his desk and pushed his glasses back on his hawkish nose. "Be that as it may, we're all extremely pleased about Estelle's—Mrs. Ackerman's—" he glanced up and smiled bleakly "—with Estelle's recovery. Bradley must have told you she's feeling so restored that she's planned a party?"

Amber nodded. "Tomorrow night."

There was short, painful pause. "Yes. Tomorrow. She thought that since the family was already gathered, as well as the board members, this would be the perfect time to officially announce your engagement. She insisted everyone stay over for one more day. Most of the board have been involved with the company almost since the beginning—thirty or forty years. They're like family—with all the good and bad that implies—and so she wanted to share the occasion with them. She has, of course, already informed everyone on the board, as well as the entire family, of your happy news."

Amber looked from Spencer to Bradley. "Can't we just tell everybody the truth before this goes any further? Surely they'll understand why we did what we did."

Both men fell silent. For a moment neither one met her gaze.

"It's not that easy, Amber," Bradley said.

"You see," Spencer interjected, "there are factions on the board who wish very much to replace Estelle as chairman. For years the loyalty and confidence of the majority of the board has rendered that impossible. But if for any reason they think the chairman has become incompetent, she would be voted out. Given some token housekeeping position."

Amber remembered the conversation she'd overheard. The company was everything to Grandy. *You know your grandfather and I made this company our life...*

Amber looked down at her lap. So the company was not only her life's work, it was all she had left of Pope Ackerman, the love of her life. If that work should be taken away from her, she'd be heartbroken. And humiliated. Amber's mind raced. What would that do to a woman like Estelle Ackerman, to be turned out or palmed off like some pathetic, useless piece of equipment?

"But she's not incompetent. We're the ones who told her I was Bradley's fiancée. Why wouldn't they believe us?"

A spasm of pain passed across Bradley's face. "I can't explain thirty years of company infighting and politics in just a few minutes, Amber, but, you see, there are several men on the board who'd love to say that Grandy was delusional, and that I'm just trying to cover that up because I want Grandy—or someone who agrees with her vision for the company—to keep the chairmanship. After all, she was the only one knew about our..." Bradley paused and sighed. "Our engagement. If we'd told anyone else, if anyone had ever even seen us together before, it might be different. More believable."

"So you're saying—"

"There are board members who'll say she just dreamed that I told her you and I are engaged, and that when I found about it, I just went along so she wouldn't look incompetent. In other words, she's crazy and I'm a liar."

"But there's another possibility," Spencer said, "and this is what frightens us the most. The revelation of your duplicity might shock Estelle terribly. It's no secret that for years she has wanted Bradley to settle into marriage and a more traditional life-style. The sudden disappointment, coupled with the irreparable damage to her reputation might be more than her heart could stand."

Amber saw a hint of the anguish she'd seen in Spencer's eyes when he'd sat alone in the ICU hallway. So, not only was there a distinct possibility that they would discredit Grandy, it was also possible that if they told her the truth, it might just kill her.

She began to see the implications of what they'd done.

Spencer leaned forward. "When Estelle was taken suddenly ill, there was an emergency board meeting. I am now acting chairman. Of course, since she's out of the hospital again, everyone knows that title is meaningless. She is once again running the company."

Bradley stood and began to pace. "We just need a little time to sort this out." Bradley faced Amber. "But in order to buy that time . . ."

Amber finally got it. "We have to pretend to be engaged."

Both men were silent.

"Does your family know that I work here?"

"They do now," Bradley said. "When Grandy was still in the hospital, she asked a lot of questions about you." He smiled, but without joy. "She was really taken with you. Anyway, she wanted to know how we met. I told her you worked here."

"That's why you told Zita that if any of your family showed up—"

"Right," Bradley said. "It's not likely, but it's possible that my fath—that someone might come by to...visit with you."

Amber saw the look of dread that passed between Spencer and Bradley and wondered at it. "What do you think we should do?"

Spencer opened his hands. "Well, this is what we thought. First we must get past the party tomorrow night, then for the next few weeks, Bradley can request that all your time here be devoted to working exclusively with him on the South American contracts we're negotiating."

Bradley spread his hands. "I really do need help. We were going to hire extra contract people, anyway. This'll keep you away from anyone asking nosy questions."

Spencer steepled his fingers. "This whole thing will eventually die down, board elections will pass, and you and Bradley can break off your engagement amicably."

Amber's head was spinning. She wanted to help Bradley and Grandy, but there were other things to consider, too.

"What will happen to my job, once we're no longer officially engaged?"

Bradley's face was suddenly serious. "You have my word, Amber. Your job here is safe for as long as you care to stay."

He took his seat again. "I'm really sorry about this. I never thought at the time that anything like this would happen."

"I know," she said. "I didn't, either." She looked down at her hands folded in her lap.

The jeans she wore were her favorites, soft and nearly white from hundreds of washings. Like most of her clothes they were old friends, but were they suitable for an engagement party to someone like Bradley Ackerman? She remembered her fantasies about him—spending a lifetime at his side. This was probably as close to the real thing as she'd ever get. Was she prepared, she wondered, even for a visit to his world?

"I don't know how to say this," she began.

Bradley leaned toward her. "What? Please, Amber, say whatever you want. And if you have to say no, that's okay. I know what I'm asking is way out of line. I wouldn't blame you at all if—"

"It's not that."

"Please, Amber," Spencer said. "Speak up. Be honest."

"I want to help, but—" She looked up. "I don't know if I have—I mean, what am I supposed to wear?"

The tension in the room broke, and Bradley shot up from his seat. "Then you'll do it?"

Amber nodded. "I'll do it."

She wanted to wish herself away from them so she could be alone to sort out her emotions. She wanted to help Bradley—after all, from the moment she'd seen him, he'd never left her thoughts. She wanted to help Grandy because, of all of them, Grandy would suffer the most because of the lie Amber and Bradley had told.

And what about her own family? Violet was already concerned, and Scarlet would, of course, be furious. But if Daddo and her mother found out what they were doing it would worry them sick.

Amber had a sudden sense of dread that things had gotten out of control and that a force had been set in motion that wasn't going to be easy to stop. Maybe there really was something to this destiny thing, she thought, but maybe it wasn't exactly what Amber had envisioned.

Bradley fumbled with his wallet and took out a platinum card. "Take this," he said. "You can go shopping tomorrow and get whatever you need. It'll just be casual. Or you could go now. It's Sunday, but surely the Galleria's still open."

Amber didn't reach for the card. "No, thank you. I couldn't go shopping tomorrow because I have class. It's the third week of the semester, and I can't skip. Besides, I can't afford to shop at the Galleria and I couldn't pay you back. And anyway, if you're supposed to have fallen in love with me, wouldn't it be because of who I really am? I can't pretend to be the kind of person who shops there, Bradley. I couldn't pull it off for five minutes. Your family would see through that right away."

"She's got a point, Brad."

He sighed. "I wish you'd take it, anyway. In case you change your mind."

She laughed a little. "I'm afraid I might, and then you'd be sorry."

He grinned at her, admiration naked on his face. "You're really something, you know."

"Yeah," she said. "I do." She stood. "Can I have the rest of the day off? I'm not entitled to any vacation yet, and I promise I'll make up the time, but I have some serious panicking to do, and I need to go home and get right on it."

"Please," said Bradley, "take whatever time you need. Don't worry about making it up. You're doing us—"

"No," Amber said. "I want to. I think for the rest of my life I'm going to be scrupulously honest."

Bradley looked slightly stricken, but he obviously saw the twinkle in her eye, because he grinned again. "Just a second." He took some paper from Spencer's desk and scrawled on it. "These are all my numbers. Office, home, fax, cellular phone. If you need me at any time, night or day, please call me."

Amber nodded. "Thanks."

"I'll call you tomorrow to get directions to pick you up."

Amber felt another worm of dread. He was coming to her house. "What time is the party?"

"Six-thirty. It's just a buffet, we're not sitting down."

"Six-thirty. Right." She stood.

"I'll walk you to your truck."

"Thanks."

Amber turned to Spencer. "I suppose I'll see you tomorrow night, then?"

He nodded and smiled at her. "Try not to worry. I know everything will be just fine."

"I hope so."

They left Spencer once again standing at his window—a solitary figure, hands clasped behind his ramrod-straight back—staring out past the endless miles of traffic lights and convenience stores.

At the door Bradley stood aside for Amber to walk out in front of him. They walked silently past the ancient pottery and artworks in their Plexiglas cases, past the shimmering pastel ladies gazing knowingly from under their parasols. Amber wanted to say something, but all her thoughts were in chaos. What would she say to Bradley's family? Would she have to tell more lies? She hated that. She wasn't even sure she could do it.

"Bradley?"

"Yes?"

"I'm afraid."

He smiled wryly. "Me, too."

They stood at the elevator, and Amber gazed up at him. "I hate lying. I always used to get caught when I tried it, so I gave it up when I was about eight."

He smiled down at her, and his green eyes warmed. "We won't stay long. In fact, I'll arrange it so that we're only there for a couple of hours. It won't be hard since Grandy just got out of the hospital and we're going crazy here—"

"And I have early classes."

"Right. Grandy was just so impressed by you she wants to show you off to the rest of the family. I think somehow she got it in her head that she picked you out for me or introduced us or something. That's the way she's telling it, anyway."

"What? How did she—"

"I don't know. I'm crazy about the old gal, but she likes to take the credit for just about anything good that happens."

Amber couldn't help smiling. Even if it was a charade the two of them were playing out, he still implied that being engaged to her would be a good thing. Too bad it was only make-believe, she thought, and her smile faded.

The elevator doors opened, and Amber was glad to step away from him. Every minute she spent with him, more and more, she found herself wanting to put her arms around him—to once again curl against his strong, broad chest. She wanted another kiss like the desperate one they'd shared at the hospital. The strangest thing was that she was certain he wanted the same thing.

She recognized the hungry way he looked at her mouth, the way his gaze caressed the line of her throat. When they were at Harlow's, she'd seen the appreciative, lingering glances at her bare shoulders. And her bodice.

Why then, she wondered, did he act as if she'd break if he touched her? An ugly thought slithered through her mind. Did he think she wasn't good enough? Not nearly sophisticated enough for his life-style? She glanced at him. No, surely, not. But then again, you never knew. Money, huge amounts of money, separated their worlds. She made a conscious effort and didn't sigh.

Zita's eyes bulged when Amber and Bradley stopped in to say that Amber would be gone for the rest of the day. Amber knew by the time she got home there would be a message on her machine demanding a complete, detailed explanation. When they reached her truck, he took the keys and unlocked the door, and Amber dropped her purse on the seat.

"Well," she said. "I guess I'll talk to you tomorrow."

"When will you be home?"

"Three-ish."

"I told Grandy that we couldn't expect your parents because your dad hasn't been very well, and that we hadn't even told them yet."

Amber nodded. "That was a good idea." She had a terrifying thought. "She won't call them, will she? Or have someone else do it? I mean, it would really—"

"No," Bradley said. "For one thing she doesn't even know their names."

Amber sagged with relief. "That's good."

He held her keys out, and when she reached for them he took her hand in his and pressed it against his chest. Amber recognized a parade of painful emotions in the intensity of his gaze and the set line of his mouth. Warmth poured through his touch, if not reassurance. Intuition told her that the touch was meant to comfort, to apologize and to thank her for what she was putting herself through to help him. And Grandy.

She accepted those things because she knew they were due her. She wished, though, that he held her hand against his heart because that's were he wanted her to be—closest to him, safe in the protection and affection he had to offer.

He gave her hand one last squeeze. "You know, I said you were my angel, and I meant it."

"I'm glad to help."

She turned her face up to him. He was looking down at her mouth. He wanted to kiss her, she could see desire darkening in his eyes. He stood close—so close she could feel the warmth of his body. In another moment she would have reached for him, but before she could move he closed his eyes, and in the space of a few seconds Amber saw him fight and win an inner war. He raised her hand to his face and kissed her fingers lightly. "You're too good to be true," he said.

Amber looked up solemnly. "That's a nice way of saying you don't believe in me."

"Not at all," he said. "You're not what I don't believe in." He turned her hand over and pressed the keys into her palm. Then he stepped away, and that small distance broke the spell of intimacy. Amber slid into the driver's seat.

"Lock your doors," Bradley said. "I'll call you at three tomorrow."

Amber lifted her hand to wave, and he backed away as the engine coughed to life. Bradley watched until the little truck disappeared out of sight up the exit ramp, then he returned to Spencer's office. The old lawyer looked up as Bradley walked in, took off his glasses and rubbed his eyes.

"She's gone?"

Brad nodded.

Spencer reached in his desk drawer and took out a bottle of bourbon and two glasses. "We weren't completely honest with your friend."

"I know. But there was no point in scaring her. I'm sure I can figure something out. I just need a little time."

"She's finished here, Bradley."

He reached out, accepted the glass and took a mouthful of the dark, fiery liquid. "I know."

"Of course we'll be able to find her something somewhere else. We all have plenty of connections, and—"

"It has to be a night job. She goes to college during the day."

Spencer sat back. "That, I'm afraid, is going to be hard."

"Tell me about it."

Spencer lifted the bottle, offering Bradley another drink. Bradley raised his palm in refusal. He needed to keep a clear head in the coming days. He told Spencer what Amber had said at Harlow's—her aspirations, her relief at finally making progress toward her life's goal.

"You know, Spence, in a way I think she knows it's over as far as working here is concerned. She seemed pretty subdued just now. But something tells me she probably would have done it, anyway—help Grandy, I mean. I think Amber's one of those rare people who are just really good. Really decent."

"I pulled her personnel file as soon as I got here today. I didn't want anyone . . . anything to happen to it."

The two men exchanged knowing looks.

Spencer lifted his desk blotter, pulled out the file and offered it across his desk. "She's a remarkable young woman. Very bright. Very pretty."

Bradley reached out and took the file. "Yeah," he said. "That doesn't surprise me. We Ackerman men seem to have an uncanny talent for attracting extraordinary women." He looked up. "And then hurting them."

Spencer didn't reply, and Bradley set the heavy crystal highball glass down on his desk. "Now," Bradley said, changing the subject as smoothly as he could. "Can you tell me what's going on with Mo and Theron and Grandy?

There's been a regular parade through the library at her house, but no one seems inclined to fill me in. I know she's been on the phone to both of my sisters, too. Hell, my father's even been called in to see her, and we both know how often *that* happens."

Spencer looked down. "I can't say anything, Brad. Estelle is making some adjustments with her own personal property, her own stock. It's strictly private."

Bradley's fist tightened until his knuckles cracked, but he managed to keep his tone calm. "And you don't think that has anything to do with me? And what about the company? Do you know if she's decided to retire? Is she trying to swing votes from Scarritt and the others to back me as chairman. Is that why she's pushing this engagement party thing—to prove to them I've settled down? What's going on, Spence? I have a right to know."

Spencer's expression was grave to the point of torment. "Don't do this, Bradley. You know I'd tell you if I could, but Estelle is, after all, still the chairman. She also has a right to conduct her private affairs as she sees fit." He paused. "She is competent, Brad. I don't know what happened last Friday, but whatever it was, it certainly didn't affect her intellect. She knows what she's doing."

Brad stood. "When am I supposed to find out what the hell's going on with the company?"

Spencer didn't answer, but gazed at Bradley with eyes blue and steady.

"I see. When everybody else does, right?" Bradley stood. "Well, I guess I'll be going. Thanks for the drink."

Spencer stood and walked around the desk. He faced Bradley for a moment, then held out his hand. Slowly Bradley reached out took it, and then each man threw a rough hand over the other's shoulders. They had been soldiers in the same war for years. They'd had their fights—old general with young general—but they loved and respected each other even when they disagreed.

"Well," Bradley said, "I'll be in my office until at least midnight. I've had another fax from Manuel."

"How's it looking?"

Bradley shrugged. "Not great. Nobody likes dealing with a company in transition, and it's hard to convince them everything's fine when I'm in the dark myself. I really need to go down there."

"Yes. You probably do."

Spence walked with Bradley out into the atrium. Pale, green light filtered through Grandy's jungle foliage and softened the hard edges of the stone walls. Bradley often thought the soaring space had the same cool, solemn aspect as a church. Or a tomb.

"Have you spoken with Tovah?"

Bradley ground his jaw. "This morning."

"It didn't go well." Spencer's words were not a question.

"No."

"Does she know the truth?"

Bradley gave Spencer a wry look. "Of course not. You know what she's like." He shrugged. "I think she wants to remarry the polo player, and she was using me to make him jealous."

"And your mother? Has she settled down any?"

"You know Blanche." He slipped into his deepest Deep South accent. "'Ambah? Ambah Who? I do declah, Bradley Alan, yo goin' to break mah haht.'" He shrugged. "Anyway, she's pretty occupied with Suzette and all that impending baby stuff."

They spoke about family business for a few moments, and then Spencer went back into his office and Bradley walked toward his corner of the building. His mind immediately returned to Amber.

Every time he thought of her, he felt an uncomfortable ache. He couldn't understand his reaction to her. He liked her. Quite a lot, in fact. But it seemed he always felt deeply disturbed after spending time in her presence. It was because of all the trouble that had been set in motion from the first time they'd been together.

Well, not exactly the first time. He sighed. He and Tovah had practically run her down trying to get to the party that day. Even though that was weeks ago, he remembered that day vividly.

She'd looked fresh and pretty and so young in her jeans with her ponytail swinging like a tassel. She'd said something to him as he got off the elevator, but he couldn't remember what. Then he saw her again later that night.

Vegetables, she'd said, standing in the galley kitchen, with eyes huge and startled.

Yes, from the moment he'd first seen her she'd been dancing somewhere on the fringe of his subconscious. And then she just happened to be the one to drive into the garage when he'd been desperate to get the hospital. Now that was really odd, he thought. Life is full of strange coincidences. She'd looked delicious that day—tanned, shining hair, scrubbed skin. He wasn't sure she recognized him, since they'd only run into each other that one time late at night.

He thought of the one kiss she'd given him. Or, rather, allowed him to take. His breath came out heavily. He'd really felt uncomfortable after that scene. And every time he'd thought of her or been around her since then, he'd felt disconcerted and out of sorts. She makes my head throb, he thought.

That's not your head throbbing, sneered the inner voice. *At least not...*

Enough, he thought, and strode purposefully toward his door. They would all struggle through the next couple of days. He and Spencer would figure something out to help Amber find another job, and then she'd be out of his life and safely away from him and his family for good.

When he reached the door to his office, Bradley paused and looked around. The atrium was silent. He frowned. For a moment he could have sworn he heard someone laughing.

Chapter Seven

"How did you get yourself into this?" Violet's voice, usually so serene and reasonable was shaking. Even though they were speaking over the phone, Amber had a vivid mental image of her oldest sister's appearance at that moment. Her creamy skin would be flushed and her black eyes snapping with outrage. "You've got to tell the truth right away, Amber. These things only get worse and worse."

"It's not that easy, Vi."

Amber tried to explain Grandy's uncertain health as well as her precarious position in the company she'd spent a lifetime building. She tried to make her sister see that revealing what she and Bradley had so innocently done could irreparably damage several lives.

"So what happens to you when all this is over?"

"Bradley promised I'd have a job at Ackerman for as long as I wanted."

Violet's silence spoke volumes.

"I believe him, Vi."

"So you won't even consider being honest?"

"Well, I might have, but it's too late. When I got home today, there was a message on my machine from Grandy. She called to apologize for the short notice about the party, but she said since this was the one time the family was gathered—"

"She sounds a little bit manipulative, if you don't mind my saying it."

"Oh, Vi. It's not that. She hasn't got any idea we're not really engaged. She just wants to share the happy news with her family."

"What are you going to do?"

"Well, I'll probably stay up all night long in a complete panic and fall asleep during class tomorrow. Then I'll have a bad hair day and a wreck on the way home."

"You said Bradley's supposed to pick you up at your house at six tomorrow, right? Do you need me to come and help you clean house and figure out what to wear?"

Amber wished she could put her arms around her sister. "If you didn't have to drive all the way from Galveston, I'd say yes, but I think I'll be okay. But you may have to come share liquid tranquilizers on Tuesday."

"Just let me know."

"There is one thing you could do..."

"What's that?" Violet's voice turned coolly suspicious.

"Would you mind telling Scarlet for me?"

"Good grief, Amber, why do you want to tell her? She'll probably go ballistic and make life hell for you."

"I want her to know, that's all. But I don't want to be the one to tell her. Right now I'm just not up to a tirade, but you know, after she settles down, she has really good ideas sometimes."

"All right, but you'd better brace yourself. She may land on your doorstep like an incoming bomb."

"I know. I'd better go. Love ya."

"Love you, too."

At nine-thirty that night Amber's phone rang. For a moment she considered letting her answering machine take the call, but that seemed ridiculously cowardly. Obviously Scarlet knew Amber was home, and if she had something to say to her older sister, she'd leave it in a lengthy and vitriolic message. At the last moment Amber decided she wasn't going to be bullied. Besides, she thought, she'd just as soon listen to the tirade once and have it over with than put it off and later on have to sit through a half-hour recording of Scarlet's creative invective.

She snatched up the receiver and forced briskness into her tone. "Hello."

"Amber?"

"Bradley?"

"You sound busy, is this a bad time?"

Amber dropped all briskness from her tone. "Oh, no. I was just cleaning house. I think my voice sounded...funny because I wasn't sure how many times the phone rang."

"Oh."

A few awkward moments passed during which Bradley said nothing. Amber began to wonder if he'd changed his mind about the reason he'd called her. "Was there something special, or—?"

"No, not really. I just thought I'd get directions to your house tonight. Tomorrow is probably going to be a crazy day."

"Are you afraid I'm going to chicken out?"

"Actually, I wouldn't blame you if you did. And you don't even know my family yet."

They both laughed. Amber imagined the separate threads of their laughter speeding toward each other and meeting inside the intersecting fibers of the phone line, curling together and past each other—sinuously, over and under—until they became tangled into a common stream of never-ending fiber-optic energy. "You're not trying to scare me away, are you?"

"Don't be ridiculous. What would I do without you? You're the only fiancée I've got."

"Gee, it's great to be needed." Despite a wracking case of nerves, Amber found herself enjoying their light banter. There is a bond among conspirators, she thought. People engaged in shady endeavors seem to develop an instant rapport.

That's because they realize that life as they know it is about to change forever—probably for the worse.

The accusing voice in her head sounded familiar—just like Violet's, in fact. Amber ignored it.

Once again the notion fleeted through her mind that the relationship with Bradley was destined. After all, how many times do strange circumstances like this arise?

About as often as people like you are silly enough to get involved in them.

"Do you have a pen handy?" Amber asked. "I'll tell you how to get here."

She gave him directions to her little house on the far west side of Houston. Amber lived in Alief, a rather unglamorous part of Harris county, which had once been an incorporated town, until Houston—expanding like a giant amoeba—had engulfed and devoured the little bedroom community.

Bradley took the directions and repeated them. "If I have any trouble I'll call you from my car."

"Sounds good." Amber would have liked to keep him on the line for hours, but she felt oddly shy. "Well, I guess I'll see you tomorrow."

"I'll be there at six."

"At six. Okay. Good night."

"Good night, Amber."

She set the phone down easily. *Good night, Amber.* She even liked the way he said her name.

"Boy," she said aloud. "Have you got it bad."

By midnight she had the living room straightened, dusted and vacuumed. She'd also washed her hair, tried on literally everything in her closet and had come close to collapsing in tears of frustration at least three times. Finally she chose a pink crepe two-piece dress. The gold buttons were encircled with white piping, so she could wear white, open-toed sandals. Her tan relieved her of the necessity of hosiery which was best, because she'd never worn a pair of panty hose for more than ten minutes without tearing huge holes in it.

She hung the suit over the door and laid out her shoes and best straw bag. Her school outfit—sneakers, the softest, oldest jeans she owned and a Sisters Morales T-shirt—lay folded on her rocking chair. With these preparations made, there was nothing left to do but go to bed.

For the next two hours she stared at the moonlight glancing off the whirling blades of her ceiling fan and listened to the climbing rose outside her window clawing at the screen. Time crawled by, and the air conditioner hummed intermittently as it cycled off and on, trying to keep the house cool. Sleep eluded Amber far into the small hours of the morning, and over and over she wondered if there was anything else she could have done.

When she finally fell asleep, she dreamed she was dancing with Bradley at a ball, but then the clock struck midnight. Instantly surreal geysers of white paper erupted from cracks in the floor, and Bradley metamorphosed into a gigantic, red-faced Phillip Ackerman who pointed at her and shouted, "This is typed wrong. Wrong type. Wrong type."

Violins shrieked while the other dancers swirled around them wearing tuxedos and ball gowns, but Amber was suddenly barefoot and naked. She tried to flee, but there were no doors out of the ballroom—no way to escape.

And all the while the clock kept banging away.

Then the dream suddenly faded, but the banging clock turned out to be real. Amber turned over and slapped the snooze alarm. Seven-thirty. She didn't feel as if she'd slept at all. She lay there motionless while fear massed itself into her chest and expanded until it took up all her breathing room. I can't do this, she thought.

"Well," she muttered against her pillow, "it's too late to back out now."

All morning Amber stumbled from class to class in a distracted blur, and she was home by two that afternoon. Bradley had left a message confirming six as the time he'd be there.

His voice sounded worried.

By four-thirty Amber had showered and fixed her hair. Then she did more house cleaning and had to shower again. From five-thirty until six she sat perched on the edge of her couch and watched the hands of the clock on her mantelpiece creep around with excruciating slowness. She wished she could pass the time constructively, but she certainly couldn't study; she couldn't even read. She tried to watch television, but it seemed there was nothing on except tabloid talk shows and their endless sideshow of morbid idiosyncracies.

Amber thought her current story would make a likely episode.

When the doorbell sounded she jumped up, smoothed her skirt and went to the door.

She opened it, and there he was. Bradley wore tan slacks, a white shirt and a light sports jacket. He stood silently for a moment, and although his gaze didn't leave her face, she knew he was assessing her in his peripheral vision. A slow, wide grin lit his handsome features. "Hi."

"Hello."

"You look perfect."

"Thanks."

"All that's missing is the cigarette and blindfold."

She smiled wanly. "Does it show that much?"

"Probably no more than it does on me."

"Shall I get my purse, or do you want to come in for a minute?"

His brow creased. "Actually, there's something I need to—well, can I come in? We need to get going, but this won't take long."

"Sure." She stepped aside and Bradley came into her house.

Amber immediately experienced that shy feeling people get when someone they want to impress sees their house for the first time. Her furniture was an eclectic mix of her grandmother's antiques, garage sale treasures and the few nice pieces she'd saved up to buy. The walls were painted a rich blue with white enamel trim, and her houseplants brought life as well as color to the modest but pretty room.

"This is nice," he said. "It's like a real home."

Amber wondered how Bradley's place looked—designed and decorated professionally no doubt. Masculine and expensive, of course, but somehow sterile and just aching, she hoped, for a feminine touch. "Thanks. Would you like something to drink? I have some beer, I think or—"

"No, we'd better go soon, but..." He turned to her. "I guess the best way to do this is to come right out and show you. Maybe we should sit."

Amber was intrigued. "Of course." She led Bradley to the sofa. "Show me what?"

He reached into his pocket and took out a small velvet box. "I thought we'd better make this convincing, so I went by Alexander's today. I hope it fits." He shrugged. "I hope you like it...even if it is just for a little while."

He opened the box.

"Oh, my God, Bradley. Is that real?"

His face screwed into a wry smile. "Oh, yes. The women you'll be meeting today are intimately familiar with jewelry. They'd knock off a fake in an instant."

"That's the most gorgeous diamond I've ever seen."

He smiled. "I thought so, too."

The band was a plain, gold circle, but the stone looked like a star fallen to earth—a perfect blue solitaire, fracturing the light into shards of brilliant color.

Amber was aware that they had come to an awkward moment. Did she take it out of the box and slip it on her finger? Did he? Outside of her fantasies, this was the only time she'd ever been offered an engagement ring. For one heart-squeezing moment she wished this proposal wasn't make-believe. Everything was perfect—the man, the moment, the stunning jewel. Only the sentiment was fake.

Amber took the ring from the box and slid it on her finger. The band was too large, and she had to use her pinkie finger to keep it from turning.

"Too big?"

"A little, but it won't fall off."

"I wanted to ask your size, but you weren't home when I called—"

"I thought your voice sounded worried."

He picked up her left hand and held it slightly away. The afternoon sun blazed in through the patio doors and ignited the facets. Dazzling splinters of color leapt from Amber's hand. Bradley smiled ruefully. "I wish you could keep it. You deserve a boxful of diamonds for everything you're doing. And everything you've done."

Amber made a face of mock outrage. "What do you mean, you *wish* I could keep it? Of course I can keep it. I'll have it sized. Or I'll gain fifty pounds."

He looked up at her, winked and gave her hand a squeeze. Then he stood. "Shall we?"

Amber took a little breath. "Might as well."

Bradley's sleek, black convertible looked as dark and dangerous as a missile parked next to Amber's little truck. Her next-door neighbor, Mr. Burk, was loitering by his wax-leaf ligustrums with hedge clippers in hand and saucer-size eyes riveted to the car that probably cost as much as his house. Amber waved, and he flapped his hand weakly back.

Bradley opened the passenger-side door for Amber, and while he walked to his side she studied the interior. The car smelled of leather and polish, and the instrument panel was a gleaming array of dials and gauges—half of which Amber didn't recognize. Bradley threw himself into his seat, released the brake and put the car in gear. The engine turned over instantly with a growl of guttural power.

"Thank God," he muttered, and they eased down Sagemont Lane between the parked pickups and station wagons and the shouting children on bicycles and in-line skates.

Amber rested her hand on the seat beside her and gazed at the ring. Light danced from her finger. "Will you have any trouble returning it?"

"No. I have it on approval." He gave her a quick glance. "And they've got a deposit."

Amber nodded. The car was low and narrow and Bradley's arm was only inches from hers. She wished she could lean over and rest her head on his shoulder. Since he was momentarily occupied with avoiding running down her neighbors' offspring, she allowed herself to study him. His hair, thick and hanging well over his collar, was much too long to be conservative. Amber thought that this was one of the advantages of being the chairman's grandson—nobody told you when to cut your hair.

She adjusted her seat belt as Bradley navigated his way back out of the neighborhood. The subdivision hadn't existed long enough for oaks or other slow-growing hardwoods to mature and lend character to the frame and tract houses. Instead cheaper, fast-growing shade trees like Japanese tallows, pine and silver maples lined the modest streets. There were no sidewalks, and the neighborhood children skated, played ball and dodged in and out of the cars parked underneath the street lamps.

Amber hoped that some of her neighbors would be outside and would see her in Bradley's car. She waved enthusiastically at everyone she even vaguely recognized.

"What made you decide to live so far out?"

"Actually, I didn't. This house was rent property that Daddo—my stepfather—owned. After he got sick he gave me and my sisters each the equity in one of his houses. He said that in case something happened to him, he wanted to make sure we each had a place we could always call home."

He was silent for a minute. "That's important. Having a place to call home, I mean."

"I think so, too."

Amber turned away. The tone in Bradley's voice had changed, and she felt as if she'd accidentally opened a door and caught a glimpse of some private sadness. And not the sudden kind caused by family crisis, but more like a hollowing, soul-deep, ache—the kind that etches itself into a person's spirit. How odd, she thought, when it seems he has so much—looks, intelligence, money, a big family and all the material comfort money can buy.

"Where do you live?" she asked softly. Although she knew Bradley's address perfectly well, she just wanted to make conversation. She wanted to draw him away from whatever unhappiness she'd accidentally stumbled upon.

"Well, right now, I keep a high rise at San Felipe and the Loop." He looked at her and shrugged. "I don't have a real home—not like you. The only place I call home is my—the family place in the hill country. Mockingbird Ranch."

"Is that where you grew up?"

"Mostly. You should see it. It's the most beautiful place on earth—to me at least. I spent every summer there with my grandfather—Pope Ackerman."

He laughed a little, and Amber marveled at the change in him when he spoke about the ranch. Inner joy illuminated his features and drove all the sad shadows from his face. "I never wanted to leave there. I just wanted to ride horses and fish and hunt and drive around with the old man and listen to his stories."

"What a wonderful way to grow up. Like a boy's adventure story."

"Yeah, it was. But I still felt that way when I was fifteen. I never wanted to leave." He sighed. "Then the old man died."

"I'm sorry."

"Yeah," he said. "So am I." As soon as they reached the access road to the freeway, Bradley shifted gears and the black car leapt forward with a roar of barely harnessed power. He glanced at Amber. "I'm sorry if that sounded curt. But the ranch is a hard subject for me. It's owned by the whole family, everyone has shares. That's the way Pope left it. Anyway, one of the major shareholders is doing some things to the property that I don't like—cutting down the trees, damming the streams, draining the lake. He wants to put fifteen-foot game fences around it and import exotic deer. Then shoot them."

"How horrible. But wouldn't that destroy the property? Not just the way it looks but the value, too?"

"Yes," he said grimly. "It would."

"Can't the rest of you do anything? Don't you all have equal say?"

"No. It's a matter of shares. And this person owns a lot of shares."

"More than you?"

"A lot more than me." He faced her. "It's my father, Amber. It's one of the things he and I disagree about. He hates the ranch, but he won't sell his shares—not that I could afford to buy them all. He wants to—oh, well. You don't need to hear this. Anyway, Mockingbird is one of the only things in the world that's important to me. It's the only place I've ever felt was home. That ranch represents everything I ever really cared about. You can't imagine how frustrating it is not to be able to do anything to save it from him."

They drove in silence. Bradley exited the freeway and entered an older section of Houston close to Rice University. The area was called The Columbine, and was a bastion of high society and old money. Amber's heart began to thud at the sight of the broad lawns, moss-hung oaks and radio-controlled access gates. These weren't houses; they were estates. She'd seen shows about places like this on late-night television.

Bradley turned into a wide gate, bordered by brick columns. In the distance, through a long, winding avenue of sheltering oaks, Amber saw a sprawling Tudor mansion, covered with ivy and framed by ancient magnolias and sweetgum trees. Crepe myrtle in shades from violet to fuchsia added bright fountains of color to the elegant, if somber, brick, and even at a distance Amber saw huge, architectural pots of yellow roses. Bradley turned and smiled pleasantly. "I think you're going to like the house."

I think I'm going to be sick.

Amber didn't try to count the cars they passed, but she couldn't help but notice they all seemed to have foreign, hyphenated, expensive names: Astin-Martin, Mercedes-Benz, Rolls-Royce. Parked a little farther away, at least half a dozen bullet-shaped Italian sports cars clustered nose-to-tail in the circular drive. Bradley parked, set the brake and turned to her. "Ready to face them?"

Amber smiled weakly. "You go. I'll drive the getaway car."

He grinned, grabbed her hand and then leaned over and kissed her lightly just on the corner of her mouth. "Come on, it'll be fun. Like a spinal tap."

No sooner had they stepped onto the brick walkway, than the heavy varnished door swung open, and a petite girl in a black dress stood before them, one hand planted on each hip. "Well, look what the cat dragged in," she said archly.

Amber didn't want to stare, but the black dress the young woman wore was spaghetti strapped, made of extremely crushed velvet and looked at least thirty years old. Pale skin peeked through the gaping rips in her black hose, and she also wore pink socks and black, heavily scuffed steel-toed work boots. Her scarlet hair was buzzed down to a quarter inch over her ears, but stood up bright and spiky on the top of her head like an unevenly chopped bristle brush. She bounced down the steps and threw herself into Bradley's arms, copper bracelets rattling and black crystal earrings swinging wildly.

Bradley's arms encircled her. "Amber," he said. "This is my sister, Adelle. Adelle, this is Amber Oakland."

"Nice to meet you," Amber said.

Bradley's sister narrowed her eyes. "So you're the one. You know," she said, "I was supposed to be back in Carmel yesterday, but then Grandy said my brother had finally gotten himself engaged. Well, I said, this I gotta see." She bounced forward and enveloped Amber in a perfumed, jangling hug. "Welcome to our family."

Then she grabbed Amber's hand. "Holy moly, look at that rock. Aunt Lucy's going to sh—uh, want one just like it."

"Good God, Adelle, what's that thing on your back?" Bradley's voice sounded horrified.

Adelle screwed her face into a parody of confusion and made a show of trying to look over her own shoulder. "Eeeuuuw," she said. "Looks like a great big tattoo. How'd that get there?"

She pressed her mouth close to Amber's ear. "It's a press-on. Don't tell, though. I love to get them going." She turned. "Well, come on, everybody's waiting."

Adelle ran back up the steps, and Bradley took Amber's elbow and led her toward the house. Adelle held the door for them. "Come into my parlor..." she said with an impish grin.

"You're a brat," Bradley said affectionately.

Adelle, with a high laugh and rattle of bracelets, disappeared through an arched doorway to their left. Amber heard the unmistakable murmur of several dozen people engaged in polite conversation, and then Adelle's high, happy voice saying, "They're here."

Amber stood in the soaring marble foyer while Bradley shut the door behind them with echoing finality.

Chapter Eight

Bradley leaned close and took Amber's elbow. "Don't be surprised if I hover," he whispered. "And don't let any of them trick you into stepping aside for a private chat. They'll just want to pick your brain. Be enigmatic."

Amber plastered a grin on her face. "How about catatonic?"

"Perfect," Bradley said. He looked down at her. "You're gorgeous. And don't talk to any of the men, or I'll have to kill them. Remember, you're *my* fiancée. They'll just have to suffer."

She knew the flirting was only to make her feel better. Oddly enough, it worked. Amber teetered in a moment of indecision and then gave herself up to fantasy. Even if it was only make-believe, even if it would last only for the rest of that day, she was the woman Bradley Ackerman loved and intended to marry. She let that sweet pretense fill her with the radiant joy of a bride-to-be.

Bradley led her through the arched doorway and into a room roughly the size of a medieval banquet hall. Amber was distantly aware of clusters of couches—a pale archipelago of color—floating on the jewel-toned rugs scattered on dark parquet floors. The walnut paneling in the huge room might have been unbearably depressing except that each wall was the backdrop for shimmering, Impressionist watercolors, and the entire wall opposite the entry had been knocked out and replaced with floor-to-ceiling glass that overlooked a sweeping lawn tilting down to a little stream and gardens ablaze with summer colors.

Everyone in the room was suddenly silent, and Amber felt dozens of pairs of curious eyes studying, calculating and comparing her to every woman Bradley Ackerman had ever dated. She almost quailed, then Bradley slipped his hand down and threaded his fingers through hers. "All the men are hating me right now," he murmured, and his breath warmed her neck. "They'd do anything to be me."

He squeezed her hand, and his strength and reassurance flowed into her through the touch. She knew she wouldn't be abandoned for one instant and that he would see that nothing unpleasant happened. She smiled up at him, and he led her forward.

Then the crowd parted and Estelle Ackerman appeared, tiny but regal in sapphire blue and leaning on a black, silver-headed cane, which Amber instinctively knew she carried only for dramatic effect. Or to whack people who irritated her.

Bradley led Amber through the guests and straight up to his grandmother. Although he nodded or smiled as he passed through the impeccably dressed crowd, he didn't stop to speak until he reached Grandy. "Well," he said, leaning down to drop a kiss on her cheek, "I hope you're pleased with yourself."

Grandy lifted her cheek to him and then turned to Amber. "My dear," she said spreading her arms to be hugged. "Please forgive me for doing this to you, but I couldn't resist."

Amber put her arms around the tiny woman and at once felt the energy and vitality burning in the small frame. "You look wonderful," she said. "It's good to see you up and around. Everyone was worried."

"I know. I really enjoyed the fuss." Grandy smiled wickedly. "Even though it was just a publicity stunt. Now I know it's awfully rude, but I want you sit right here with me. We'll make everyone come and talk to us." She turned to her grandson. "Well, I think I've waited long enough, I'd like a drink. Would you like some wine, Amber? Good. A glass of wine for your fiancée, Bradley, and I'll have the usual."

Amber allowed herself to be led to an immense floral couch flanked with flower-laden end tables and high-backed chairs. Bradley, obviously feeling Amber was safe with his grandmother, disappeared to get them drinks. Across the room she caught Spencer Bailey watching her gravely, but once again, just as at the emergency room, she thought she detected a hint of satisfaction in his look.

As soon as they sat, Bradley's relatives came to be introduced. She met Uncle Mo's wife, Lucy, who eyed Amber's ring with naked envy, and Theron's wife, Bonnie, a sweet, powdered donut of a woman. There were cousins and board members, and Judge Finis Ewing from the Fifth Circuit, one of Pope's oldest friends. And, no matter who tried to entice him away, Bradley stood at her shoulder like one of the Royal Household Guards, and slowly nursed a stiff-looking bourbon and water.

Blanche Ackerman appeared aflutter with worry because of an upsetting phone conversation with Bradley's pregnant sister. She presented her cheek for her son to kiss, then perched momentarily on the chair by Amber. "Our poor Suzette's been bedridden since her fifth month," she confided. "She's just stricken that she can't be here today. Poor thing can't even sit up. I'm mortally terrified I won't be there when the blessed moment occurs. Oh, honey, look at that pretty ring. We're all just ecstatic for Bradley. Y'all have to come for supper soon. Have y'all set a date yet? No? Oh, you coy things."

She sat for only a moment, then she was off to worry some more—a pretty, if dithery, little woman smelling of White Shoulders. Amber wondered if Bradley's father was going to appear.

Grandy, who had been engaged in a discussion of the merits of West Texas light crude, leaned toward Amber. "I wasn't going to ask, but since my daughter-in-law did... You haven't set a date?"

"No. Not yet. I'm in the middle of school, and Bradley's so busy with the company—"

"Hah. I wouldn't let that stop me."

Bradley leaned over. "We're going to enjoy our engagement, Grandy. There's no rush."

Amber was immediately aware of a sly look in the old woman's eye. "Well, I think that's ridiculous. I only knew Pope for three weeks before we got married."

"Here we go," Bradley muttered. "It's family legend time."

Grandy looked up, completely unruffled and obviously determined to tell her story. "I was seventeen years old, and Pope was driving all over Louisiana and East Texas buying up oil and gas leases. In those days all it took was cash and a handshake. Now, my father owned a few thousand acres in the Big Thicket, and Pope came through and leased them. While they were talking I brought him a glass of lemonade—"

"It was corn liquor," Bradley said. "Ask her about her father's still."

"Who's telling this?" Grandy snapped, but her eyes were twinkling. "Anyway, we talked for an hour. He came back through the next week and we talked again. Then the following Saturday he drove up while I was hanging laundry for my mama, and he said, 'Estelle, are we getting married today or not?' And I said, 'Well, make up your mind or my clothes won't get dry.'" She laughed aloud, enormously entertained by her own story. Then her smiled faded softly and her voice grew wistful. "We were married for thirty-five years."

Amber was wondering what to say, when she became suddenly aware that Bradley had become tense and vigilant. She looked toward the door just in time to see Phillip Ackerman standing triumphantly in the doorway. He hadn't come in alone.

Next to him stood Tovah Stein.

Amber didn't know where to look. She didn't want to stare, but she felt as if someone had just walked into the room displaying a loaded gun. She was also aware of the intake of scandalized breath and ripples of nervous movement—elbow nudging, eyebrow lifting and the sudden halting of glasses raised only partway to open mouths. From the corner of her eye she caught people glancing from her to Tovah, from Phillip to Bradley. Amber decided to take her cue from Grandy, and had she not been watching, she might have missed the almost imperceptible narrowing of bright blue eyes and the way the small hand tightened around the Austrian crystal glass.

"Well, look who's here," Grandy said, setting down her drink and reaching for her cane. "Help me up, dear," she said to Amber without taking her eyes from the couple at the door. "It's just who I've been waiting for."

Although Grandy stood, she made no move to walk toward her eldest son. Amber saw their gazes lock and then engage in a silent struggle. Phillip was the first to look away, acting as if he'd suddenly seen someone across the room who needed to be acknowledged. Tovah stood, icy and stunning, in silver-gray D'Avalinni with matching snakeskin pumps.

Phillip tried to take Tovah's elbow, but she snatched it away, giving him a look of freezing dismissal. Then the two of them walked forward.

Phillip didn't kiss his mother, and she didn't offer her cheek to Tovah. "Hello, Mother dearest," Phillip said. Amber recognized the bravado in his tone. She knew instantly that Phillip was afraid of Grandy. Or of what she could do. Despite his outrageous behavior, there was a wariness in his attitude, like the slyness of an ill-mannered child who's not quite sure how far to push his luck. He turned to Bradley.

"And here's the lucky man. And the lucky girl. Introduce us to the lucky girl, Bradley."

The two men didn't reach out to each other, but Amber feared she would be expected to shake Phillip's hand. She knew he was just the kind of person who would crush her fingers or make an obscene gesture in her palm. She almost shuddered. What, she wondered, happens to a man or a family to cause this kind of animosity? And why would Phillip bring Tovah here? What would possess him to deliberately hurt and embarrass so many people?

"Amber," Bradley said, in a voice that sounded exactly like a warning growl, "this is my father, Phillip Ackerman." He turned slightly, and Amber was glad she didn't have to look at his face. "And this is Tovah Stein."

Amber looked up and braced herself for a lacerating glare. Instead she saw a starkly beautiful woman hiding hurt and bewilderment with a show of glacial control.

Oh, my God, she's in love with him. Amber smiled. "I'm happy to meet you."

"Well, Phillip," Grandy answered, "I'm glad you're finally here. We can make our little announcement now, can't we?"

Phillip's face reddened furiously, but Amber saw no lessening in his petty, vicious glee at the discomfort he was inflicting on all of them. She turned to Tovah. "This is the first time I've been in this house, and I'd really like to freshen up. Can you show me to the powder room, Tovah?"

Scarlet lips curved in a grateful, ironic smile. "Love to," she said.

"Excuse us, please," Amber said, smiling sweetly at Phillip's disappointed, slack-jawed face. She didn't look at either Grandy or Bradley.

The rest of Grandy's guests parted like the Red Sea as Tovah led Amber toward the foyer. Amber tried to present the picture of oblivious nonchalance and chatted lightly about Bradley's relatives and the stunning artwork. Tovah fell into the act, also, and touched Amber's arm companionably as they swept past the goggle-eyed guests.

Once outside the room Amber dropped the pretense and followed the elegant brunette down a little hallway and into an enormous, old-fashioned powder room. With the door closed and locked, Tovah crossed her thin arms and leaned against the pink marble countertop. Amber leaned right beside her.

"Well," said Tovah. "I wonder what they're talking about in there."

Despite raw nerves, Amber chuckled. Then the two of them sat there silently for a few moments side by side. Amber realized Tovah was studying her face, aching with unasked questions, but too proud to play the heartbroken, jilted lover.

Amber wanted to ask how Tovah happened to come in with Phillip Ackerman and what had transpired between Tovah and Bradley, but there were questions that she, too, simply couldn't ask. To Amber it seemed that this information, though unsaid, was still communicated. She also felt it somehow leveled the ground between the two women. *You have your secrets, I have mine.* Amber knew that the two of them would probably never be friends, but from that moment on they would certainly be equals. Tovah obviously didn't remember seeing Amber in the elevator, and Amber decided not to mention it.

"Well," Tovah said finally, "I don't know what I was expecting, but I wasn't expecting you."

Amber knew no insult was intended, and Tovah's words didn't offend her. "I don't know what to say. I know that you and Bradley have been . . . friends for a long time."

Tovah smiled ruefully. "Well, we've known each other all our lives, but I don't know if you'd call us friends anymore."

Amber met Tovah's dark, sad gaze. "I think that would disappoint him."

Tovah didn't answer, and Amber saw her eyes growing bright and wet. She also knew if she touched her or offered too much sympathy, tears would come, embarrassing to Tovah and impossible to hide when they rejoined the others. "Come on," she said briskly. "Let's go back before they send a rescue party for one of us."

Tovah smiled, and her old sassiness reappeared. "I wonder which one it would be."

When they rejoined the others, Amber saw Bradley standing close to the door and talking with Spencer. Without making too much of a fuss, he disengaged himself from the conversation and walked toward Amber. Tovah gave Amber's arm a squeeze. "Give Bradley my love," she said. "Right now I need a Scotch." As Bradley approached, she contrived to be looking away so they didn't speak.

Bradley took Amber's left hand in his and dropped his other arm around her shoulders. Had they truly been lovers, the gesture would have been sweet but insignificant. However, as soon as Bradley's hand touched hers, Amber's blood raced. He stood so close her shoulder was pressed into his chest and the whole left side of her body molded to his.

"That," he said, "was the bravest thing I've ever seen anyone do." Then he raised her hand and kissed her fingertips. "You're a constant surprise, Amber Oakland."

Amber tilted her face up. He was gazing directly into her eyes, and the touch of his hand and the undisguised admiration on his face swirled inside her, awakening nerve endings and secret hopes. Again, she knew he wanted her. Why, she wondered, why does he hold himself back? She could tell he wanted to kiss her. And more. She could feel the desire vibrating between them like music or a static charge.

She parted her lips and saw how the sight made him ache. He was losing control. She saw him wavering and leaning closer, the unmistakable crumbling of his resolve and the darkening of his skin with desire....

"Everybody," Grandy called from the center of the room.

Bradley grimaced as if he'd been struck. Or suddenly and rudely awakened. He gave Amber's hand one last squeeze, then released her. Then he turned, clasped his hands behind his back and faced his grandmother. Although probably the smallest person in the room, she commanded instant attention.

She turned toward Bradley. "Everyone knows why we're here," she said, "and by now you've all met Amber, whom we all think is a marvelous girl—"

"And way too good for you, buddy," a deep, good-natured voice called.

Grandy laughed along with the others, but held her hands out commanding silence. "It's time to admit that some of us have played a little trick on you, Brad. For the last two days your family has been conspiring behind your back."

Amber glanced up and saw him frown slightly, but he was obviously amused and content to let the proceedings go on.

Grandy reached behind her and took an envelope from Theron. She cleared her throat. "For years I've known—we've all known—what the desire of your heart is. We all know, too, that this is probably what your grandfather would have wanted . . ."

Amber saw his eyes widen almost imperceptibly and the slightest tightening of his jaw.

"And although this may be little bit early, it's the one time your entire family is gathered together since we've scattered to the four winds. But without further ado," Grandy said, "it's my utmost pleasure to present to you and Amber, from your family, and as our wedding present to you both, the deed to Mockingbird Ranch."

Chapter Nine

Amber thought she and Tovah had pulled off a remarkably convincing act when they'd left the party together earlier. Once Grandy's announcement left her lips, however, Bradley launched into a tour de force worthy of an Academy Award.

All the rest of the guests beamed and clapped politely; only Amber stood close enough to see the vein in his neck throb. Only Amber heard the muttered epithet and saw the sudden stab of anguish darken his green eyes.

He put his arm around her shoulders and pressed his face to her ear. The others would see it as a kiss. "Just go along with me," he said urgently. "We'll work this out later."

She faked an enormous smile. "Of course," she whispered through her teeth.

He took her hand, led her through the happily grinning guests and accepted the envelope. Then he turned and faced the center of the room.

"Everybody here knows what this means to me, so I don't have to make a mushy speech. But I want you to know I love you all." He paused, and a devilish gleam appeared in his eye. "And I also want you to know you have a week to get all your personal stuff off my property before I throw it in the Blanco River."

Everyone laughed except Phillip who eyed his son with undisguised resentment. Amber saw the look returned and knew that Bradley was only kidding when he told the others to take their personal effects from Mockingbird. When it came to Phillip, however, he was deadly serious.

"Now," Grandy said, "everyone, please enjoy yourselves. Bradley tells me we can't keep Amber any longer because of her early classes." She looked up and gave him a sly smile. "But I think they just want to be alone." Then she turned toward a waiter who'd appeared, pushing a cart laden with tinkling glassware. "Lars," she said, "please serve." And the white-jacketed man picked up a tray of crystal flutes, which quickly found their way into the hands of the guests.

Bradley gave Amber a glass and took one himself. He smiled, but his eyes were sad and filled with apology.

Grandy lifted her drink. "To Bradley and Amber."

"Bradley and Amber," murmured the others, and dozens of glasses touched and chimed. Amber tapped Bradley's glass with hers and sipped the cool, sparkling champagne. Over the rim of her glass she saw Phillip Ackerman staring at her.

The corner of his mouth lifted in a sardonic leer, and his cold, green eyes glittered with satisfaction. Obviously he didn't feel defeated by Grandy's announcement. Fear slid up Amber's spine like the blade of a knife.

He knew something they didn't know.

The party was beginning to break up, and the next moments passed in a blur of well-wishing, dinner invitations and murmurs of "We have to get together soon." Amber was kissed and hugged and exclaimed over with such warmth and acceptance, she had to struggle to hold back her tears. Soon most of the guests departed.

The magic ball was over. Time to go back to her real life.

Spencer was the last to approach them, and Amber saw Bradley's demeanor chill. "Spence," he said quietly, even as he took the older man's hand, "you should have told me."

"I couldn't, Brad." He gave them both an apologetic look. "I gave my word."

Bradley's mouth tightened, and Amber knew he faced an inner struggle. How can you fault a man for being true to his word? After all, if Bradley had been completely honest, he wouldn't be in this fix.

"There's more, Bradley. The envelope Estelle gave you is empty. The real agreements are in the library. She wanted me to give you and Amber executed copies to read later." He looked at Amber. "You may want to have your family lawyer look it over."

Bradley gave him an incredulous look. "What the hell are you talking about, Spence? You know what's going on here."

"Yes, I do," he said quietly. "But you don't. You need to read that agreement."

Bradley nodded. "All right. And another thing, who bought the shares? There's no way Suzette and Mo and everybody else would just give away their interest in Mockingbird. Not to mention my father. Who paid for this?"

Spencer glanced around the room. Bradley's uncles and their wives were saying goodbye to some of the board members. Tovah had slipped out sometime earlier, and Adelle and some of the cousins had walked out to enjoy the evening in Grandy's magnificent, sculpted garden. "We can't talk here," he said. "I'll get the papers from the library, and we can meet at the office. Maybe you should tell Estelle you're leaving."

They found Grandy seated among her friends and family. She rose and kissed them both and gazed at her grandson with a look of tender affection. "Pope would have loved this."

"I know," he replied.

"You've made me very happy, Bradley." She looked at Amber. "She's a marvelous girl."

"I know that, too." He gave her a look of exaggerated consternation. "What have you been up to, Grandy? How'd you pry Mockingbird out of my father's hands?"

Grandy looked up at him, suddenly frail and weary. "Oh, son, don't make me go into that now. I have guests, and I'm tired, and I . . . I don't feel very well. Let's just enjoy the evening, please."

"All right." He patted her hand. "I have to take Amber home now, but I'll call you tomorrow."

"It'll have to be late in the day. I have appointments all morning," she said. "I'm supposed to see my new doctor at noon."

Bradley gave her a hard but affectionate look. "You shouldn't be drinking, you know. I'm going to tell on you."

"Just a sip doesn't hurt," she replied. "Besides—" she looked at Amber warmly "—this is all I need to make me feel good. Knowing that you've found a wonderful girl and you're going to be happy."

Amber looked away.

Spencer reappeared and gave each of them a thick manila envelope. Amber kissed him on the cheek, but Bradley said a much cooler goodbye and then took Amber back through the foyer and out the front door. The evening was soft around them, and the undulating song of cicadas rose and fell as they walked to Bradley's car. In the west, the sun was setting in a rack of purple clouds, and spears of light pierced the sky as Bradley drove through the sentinel pillars and down the drive.

Neither of them spoke.

When they were halfway to her house, Bradley reached over and took her hand. "You were wonderful tonight."

"You have a beautiful family. Such nice people—Adelle, your mother, your uncles. You're lucky."

"I know."

He smiled at her. They were treating each other gently and carefully after a grueling evening, but Amber still felt the hurt hanging in the air between them. Hers. Bradley's, too. She wondered what was in the envelopes, but she was too exhausted to think about it.

Dusk had gathered when he walked her to the door. The evening light lingered in the west, but stars had come out overhead and were winking down at them. Amber's wisteria vine canopied her front porch, and because Bradley was so tall, he had to brush away the hanging tendrils. He took her keys and unlocked her door.

"Would you like to come in?" Her words were ritual and she already knew the answer.

"I'd better not. Spence is waiting for me at the office."

She nodded—at a loss for what to say next. *I had a nice time.* Her head was beginning to ache. "Well, I'd better go in. I have some studying to do."

"You're not working this week, are you?"

"No. This is my shift off."

"Oh. Right."

Amber thought she heard disappointment in his voice. *That's just because you desperately want it to be there.*

"Before I forget, you'd better take this." She tucked her purse and the manila envelope under her arm and took off the ring. Her eyes were burning, and she was glad the porch light wasn't on.

He sighed as he took it and dropped it in his pocket.

She couldn't look up at him. "Well, good night," she said, but she didn't turn away.

"Amber," he said, and she felt his hand sliding under her hair, drawing her to him. She put her arms around his waist, and he held her and stroked her hair. His touch was comforting and gentle, and for a moment she allowed herself to feel safe and cherished and cared for, pressed there against his broad chest and held against his heart. "Sweet girl," he murmured, and he held her closer.

She looked up at him, and the last of the evening light showed the longing on his face and the hunger awakening in his body. "Amber," he said again, and his voice was a groan of desire.

He kissed her. His mouth was firm and warm, and she tasted the champagne he'd been drinking. He opened his mouth, breathing into her as he pulled her even closer and tighter against him. The kiss deepened from tenderness to desire and then to passion. His hand slid from around her back forward to cup her breast and tease the aching bud through the fabric of her dress.

She slipped her arms under his jacket and felt the rising heat in his body. The muscles at his sides flexed and expanded under her fingers as he arched himself toward her. She ached to feel his hands against her skin, and she knew that he, too, wanted their bodies pressed together without the frustration of clothing.

"Bradley," she breathed into his mouth.

With a groan he took his mouth from hers. His breath was ragged, and every tortured movement of his body told her how he wanted her, all the ways he wanted to be with her and inside her. "I'd better go," he said, but he didn't release her.

You don't have to. Stay here. Come inside.

"Spence is waiting."

"Oh, well, I guess so."

"Amber, I . . ."

Whatever it was he thought of, he didn't say. He kissed her once more on the mouth. Sweetly. Then he let her go, turned and strode away, his footsteps firm and determined.

Amber went inside and leaned against the door. She listened as his car's ignition fired, caught and roared away, taking him back to his office. Back to his world.

Although it was still early, Amber undressed and got in bed. She tried to remember every detail of the evening. She had charmed his family, shamed his cruel father and made peace with his former girlfriend. It had been a triumphant day.

She cried herself to sleep.

The next morning, groggy and red-eyed, she dressed for school. On her way out the door she saw the envelope Spencer Bailey had given her. She bit her bottom lip. Although she was curious about the contents, she knew reading the papers would probably make her feel bad. They were part of a fantasy that was now over.

She had half an hour before she had to leave, so she put water on for instant coffee and sat down to read the document. The first part was dull, dry property descriptions—boring, legal "map and plat thereof" jargon. Then she came to the conditions and stipulations. The kettle began to rumble as she skimmed the paragraphs. "What on earth . . . ?"

She read the words again, and the kettle hissed and erupted into a long, high shriek as the water inside came to a furious boil.

"Oh, my God."

"But what does it mean?" Amber asked.

Spencer steepled his fingers; Amber couldn't read his expression. Bradley's, however, was unmistakable—he was in a blind fury.

Amber had phoned the office immediately after reading the documents, and Bradley had asked that she come down right away. She was in such a state she skipped her classes, knowing her presence there would be useless with this new uncertainty hanging over her head.

"It means," Spencer said, "that if you don't marry Bradley in Estelle's presence, all the shares given to the two of you as a wedding present revert to Phillip Ackerman, giving him eighty-five percent ownership of Mockingbird Ranch. Bradley, of course, retains only his original fifteen-percent share. Estelle will therefore forfeit the cash she paid him and all her shares in the Ackerman Drilling Company."

"And Phillip gets all of them? Everything?"

"Exactly."

"But *why?*" Amber's shock and incredulity echoed in her voice. She'd been horrified ever since she'd read the terms of the agreement Grandy had signed. "Why would she agree to such a thing?"

"I don't know. Perhaps those were the terms Phillip insisted upon before he would part with his stock. Maybe he had an idea that Bradley's engagement was not real. It's possible he could be doing this to force Bradley into a marriage he hadn't really planned on. Or, if Bradley chooses not to marry he retains his freedom, but Phillip strips his mother of the company and Bradley loses Mockingbird."

Although Spencer spoke almost without inflection, his eyes held sympathy and deep regret.

"And there's something else you need to know," Bradley said. His voice was controlled, but Amber heard the anger. "My father's not going to let you work in peace here. Not after this. He's going to torment you every chance he gets, and I'm afraid there's nothing Spence or I can do to stop him."

Amber's heart labored. "Am I fired then?"

"Of course not. But you won't be able to stay here. He'll make your life hell."

She looked out the window. The high, hot sun had bleached the color from the sky, and the oaks and willows seemed bowed under the blazing onslaught. The grass looked like straw, and a slow stream of cars crawled down Gessner, trailing exhaust fumes. "Why does she insist that the wedding take place in her presence?"

Bradley shrugged. "Suzette eloped. Maybe it has something to do with that. I don't know. I don't get it, either."

"Is there some time limit on this?" Amber asked. "I mean, does the offer expire at midnight on such and such a date?"

"Not exactly," Spence answered. "The shares have now been escrowed, so the deed to the ranch is in transition. All the former shareholders have the same rights they always had. Nothing changes until the transfer is final."

"So if we don't get married, nothing will change."

"That's right," Bradley said.

"Until Estelle . . . dies. If you and Bradley aren't married to each other, upon Estelle's death the shares revert to Phillip."

"And her company shares, too?"

"Yes, and those, too."

The convoluted terms were too much for Amber to comprehend at once. She needed time to sit and think and sort out what had happened. And what to do next. But time was something she didn't have. Everything that was important to her—her job, her education, Bradley—all her dreams were disappearing like smoke on a windy day. "I can't think right now. But I suppose I'd better start looking for another job."

Bradley winced. "I'm sorry. I never thought—"

"I know."

Spencer stood and walked around his desk. "Maybe we can work something out. After all, there's no rush just yet."

At exactly that moment the phone on his desk rang. He ignored it. Moments later the intercom buzzed, and a look of irritation flashed across his face. "Excuse me," he said.

Amber glanced at Bradley. His face was awash in anger and misery.

Spencer was suddenly rigid with alarm. "What?" All the color drained from his face. "When? Where? I'm on my way." He slammed down the phone and turned to Bradley. "Estelle collapsed at breakfast. They're taking her to Burdyne."

By three o'clock that afternoon, Grandy's condition had stabilized, and Bradley was allowed in to see her. Amber waited with Spencer on the same bench they'd shared before.

Amber wondered if the rest of the family would all turn around and come back again when they heard what had happened. Or if they'd wait. Blanche had gone down to the cafeteria for coffee. Phillip, mercifully, had stayed away.

Spencer sat quietly, hands folded in his lap. Amber's heart ached for him, fearing what he might be facing. The old, she thought, have little hope of outliving their grief.

Bradley reappeared, his face pale and haggard. "She wants to see you," he said to Amber, "but her doctor says to wait. They're changing her IV."

He sat beside her, and she tried to sound hopeful. "How does it look?"

"I don't know. No one will tell me anything." He shrugged. "I guess they don't know." He turned to her, his brow more creased with worry than she'd ever seen. "When you go in to see her she's going to ask you . . ." He shook his head. "She wants us to get married. Here. Today."

Amber couldn't answer. She knew her jaw was sagging.

"I'm not surprised," Spencer said. "She's afraid she's dying. And now she's not only in pain, she's worried sick she's cost you Mockingbird and destroyed the company by signing that agreement."

"But we couldn't get married today even if we wanted to," Amber said. "The blood tests . . . the license."

Spencer looked up. "Oh, all that could be taken care of easily. Judge Ewing can arrange the license today and waive the blood tests."

"I just had one, anyway," Bradley said. "For my visa."

"I had one when the company hired me but that was a few weeks ago," Amber said. "I don't know if that counts. But I know I'm healthy." She looked down. "And besides, we're not . . . I mean . . ." Amber couldn't finish the thought and silence fell like a blanket.

She knew they were all thinking the same thing, but only she could voice the questions. "If we are married, and something does happen to Grandy, what happens to her shares of the company?"

"She has a will," Spencer said. "She decided on the disposition of her property a long time ago. That would be the controlling document concerning the drilling company assets—that is, if you and Bradley marry in her presence as stipulated. Mockingbird would go to Bradley. And to you, of course."

Amber shook her head. "I wouldn't try to keep any of it."

Bradley leaned forward. "Wait a minute, Amber, what are you thinking of? This is my family mess. It's my fault and—"

"But it's my fault, too," she said. "I'm as much to blame as you are for this. If you lost Mockingbird, and your father destroyed Grandy's company because of something I'd done, I'd hate myself." She turned to Spencer. "There's nothing in those papers saying we have to *stay* married, is there?"

He shook his head. "No."

"Well," Amber said. "We could get married for a little while. Just long enough to satisfy the terms of that paper."

"You would do that?" Bradley's voice was incredulous.

"Yes," she said. "I would. In fact, I think I'd insist on it."

He took her hand. "I've said it before, Amber. You're an angel. I've never known anyone like you."

She stood. "Do I have time to go change clothes?"

"I don't know. I'm not sure how she is or how long it'll take Judge Ewing to get here with the license."

Amber looked down. She was wearing jeans and a sleeveless white shirt. Not exactly a wedding gown, she thought. But then again it was only going to be a make-believe marriage. "Well," she said, "I'm going to go brush my hair and put on some lipstick."

Bradley stood and watched her walk away, her flaxen hair swinging against her tanned shoulders. He turned to Spence. "Why is she doing this? Putting herself in this mess for us? For me?"

Spencer gave him a hard look. "Well, if you can't figure it out..." He didn't finish the sentence, but turned on his heel, and walked away.

"What do you mean?"

Spencer turned back. "She's in love with you, Brad. Anyone could see that."

Spencer turned and left just as Bradley opened his mouth to protest. He stood looking down the empty hall, first one way, then the other. "No way," he said, and sat back down on the bench. He leaned forward to lever himself up, then changed his mind and collapsed back against the wall. He looked down the hallway where she'd gone and frowned.

"No way."

Judge Ewing arrived in less than thirty minutes. The physician on call, Dr. Prama, had agreed to act as the other witness. The four of them filed into Grandy's ICU cubicle while the nurses watched, some stony-faced with consternation, others dewy-eyed at what appeared to be the unfolding of a deeply romantic scenario.

"Estelle," Spencer said tenderly, leaning over her. "We're all here."

Blue eyes fluttered open and she smiled weakly. "I'm so happy," she said. "So happy."

Dr. Prama wrapped his small, dark hand around Grandy's wrist. "I'm sorry, but we must hurry."

Judge Ewing shoved his glasses up on his nose, opened a small book and began. "Friends, we are gathered now to witness the marriage..."

The introductory words were simple and quickly said. "Do you Bradley Alan Ackerman take Amber Louise Oakland to be your lawful, wedded wife?"

"I do."

"And do you, Amber Louise Oakland...?"

"I do."

"Is there a ring?"

Bradley slapped his coat pocket. "We had a...but it's in my safe."

"Take this one." Grandy's voice was slow and pain filled. Amber turned in time to see her pulling the gold band off her finger. One edge was worn paper-thin. "I haven't taken this off in fifty years. I hope you wear it even longer."

Amber looked up at Bradley. "I can't," she whispered.

Spencer leaned toward her. "You have to. You'll hurt her feelings."

Bradley took the ring—a small, plain circle of old gold—and put it on Amber's finger. The fit was perfect.

"Bradley, repeat after me. With this ring, I thee wed..." And then Judge Ewing said, "By the power vested in me by the State of Texas, I pronounce you man and wife. You may kiss the bride."

The kiss was quick, and Bradley's expression was joyless and guilt ridden. Grandy alone seemed happy, and she smiled through blue, watery eyes.

"I'm sorry," Dr. Prama said, "but I must ask you all to step outside now."

I'm married, Amber thought as she left the hospital room. I'm married to the man I love.

I will not cry.

Out in the hallway Bradley, Judge Ewing and Spencer stood around her silent and waiting—obviously as numb and dazed as she was. To Amber it seemed as if they were all survivors of a catastrophe—still too shocked to comprehend the extent of the damage done. She couldn't stand them looking at her. They would see how she felt. She couldn't bear their pity. *I have to get out of here.* "Bradley, I'm going home," she said. "I have to... to—"

"I understand." His eyes were glazed with pain and sadness. *I'm sorry. I'm so sorry.* "I'll walk you to your car."

"No." She looked down. "I mean, you'd better stay here, in case... in case they need you."

Amber walked out of the hospital alone. She climbed into her truck, a new bride, married to the man she loved.

She wanted to die.

As she drove west, the sun went down, setting the sky on fire and burning up the last of the day with light the color of blood. The piercing shafts caught the ring Amber now wore and turned it scarlet. As she drove down her street and past her neighbors and their children she wanted to yell at them. *How can you act like nothing's happened?* Surely they can feel this, too, she thought. Surely no one person has to feel this all alone.

She didn't even bother to undress. She unplugged her phones, crawled into bed and dragged a pillow to her chest and waited for the oblivion of sleep.

The next morning she forced herself to go to school. She concentrated on the lectures, took notes and spoke lightly to her acquaintances. No one mentioned the thin ring she now wore. Amber knew she should take it off, she just couldn't make herself. The ring was, after all, the only real thing about her marriage. That much she wanted to keep, even if only for a little while.

During her lunch break she called the hospital. The orderly who answered told her Mrs. Ackerman seemed to be holding her own. A cushion of numbness settled around her, and that afternoon when she arrived at home, she was even able to study. The house was quiet for hours. Too quiet.

Then she remembered she'd disconnected her phones. If her mother or sisters tried to call they would worry if there was no answer. She reattached the lines and reset her answering machine; within minutes the phone rang.

"Amber?"

"Bradley. How are you?"

"Okay. I'm at the hospital."

"How is Grandy?"

"I don't know."

"They won't tell you anything?"

"No," he said. "It's not that. We went down for coffee half an hour ago, and while we were gone, she got up, put on her clothes and walked out of here."

Chapter Ten

Bradley was seated at the bar when Amber walked into Harlow's. They'd decided to meet where no one they knew was likely to see them. Since it was only five-thirty, too early for the first dinner rush, the restaurant was almost empty.

He stood when she walked in and hugged her lightly. "Do you want to get a table?"

"No. This is fine."

He pulled out a bar stool for her and she sat down.

"Spencer is with Grandy now. At the house—"

"How is she? What happened?"

"Nobody knows. All the tests came back negative. Blood work, CAT scan—all of it. One minute she's in a coma—nearly dying, then the next thing you know she's completely fine—ordering people around and driving everybody crazy. There might be something wrong inside her brain, but they didn't have a chance to do all the tests. She left."

"Can't they—you . . . Can't *somebody* make her stay?"

The look he gave her was her answer. No one—not man, woman or child—could make Estelle Ackerman do something she didn't want to do.

"There's more," he said.

Amber had a familiar sinking feeling. Funny, she thought, I'm almost getting used to this. "What?"

"She's upset about the wedding. I mean, she's ecstatic that we got married, but now she's talking about a reception. A big one. A few hundred guests, a dinner dance and lots of photographers—the works. She wants us to come over tomorrow night to discuss the notices to the press. She thinks we should sit for pictures in her garden."

Amber's heart almost stopped. The press? If Maude and Daddo and her sisters found out about her marriage by reading an article in the newspaper, they'd be devastated. Her sisters would be furious. They'd never forgive her for hurting their parents. And, pretend marriage or not, she wouldn't blame them. "What are we going to do?"

"Well, I've been thinking, we've got to buy some time to come up with a plan, and I can only think of one mature and constructive way to do it."

"What's that?"

"Let's hide."

Four hours later Bradley turned into the long, winding driveway leading to Mockingbird Ranch. Amber had thrown a few things in a bag and left a message on Vi's machine, telling her that she was spending a few days in the hill country with a friend. She'd even left the phone number in case of emergencies. But not the name of her host.

After Bradley picked her up at her house, they'd driven west into a gold and vermillion sunset. He'd left the convertible top down all the way, and the wind tearing through Amber's hair had felt cleansing.

And it also relieved them of the necessity to talk.

Bradley told Amber that only Spencer Bailey knew where they would be and that he'd extracted Spencer's promise not to reveal their whereabouts. To anyone. Amber knew Spencer Bailey's word would bind him. That had been demonstrated vividly in recent days.

As the convertible rumbled over the uneven ground the headlights caught yearling deer fleeing in their leaping, jagged path, tails flagging in alarm. Nighthawks wheeled overhead, calling to each other in their rough voices as they hurtled through the mild night air hunting and devouring insects on the wing. Behind them in the purple sky rose a round, yellow Texas moon.

Bradley pulled up to the long, low house, killed the engine and turned off the lights. A silent, star-spangled night settled around them. He took a deep breath. "Smell that."

"It's wonderful. Cedar, isn't it?"

"Yeah. Cedar, pine. Mostly good, clean air. Can you hear the water?"

"I—I think so."

"Maybe we'll walk down after we put our stuff inside."

Although no lights were on, Amber could see the house was an odd design—an old stone ranch house that had been expanded upon and added to with soaring glass exposures and beams as thick and heavy as railroad ties—Colorado ski lodge meets the Old West. Quirky but still appealing, she thought.

Bradley grabbed their bags and led her to the front door. "I'll put the car up later. There's a Jeep in the garage, and tomorrow I'll show you the property. If you want to see it, I mean."

"I'd like that."

Amber knew she should be unhappy. She should be frightened, devastated and heartbroken about the bizarre and tragic turn of events of the past few days. But somehow driving into the hill country with Bradley and seeing the way this homecoming infused him with peace and joy gave her happiness, too. Hope came back to life inside her. Maybe, just maybe, things would work out after all. Maybe this marriage really was meant to be.

She looked at the heavy, varnished door, outlined in the silvery light of the moon and stars. I'm on my honeymoon, she thought. And this is our threshold. Somehow she knew Bradley was thinking the same thing.

He set down their bags, found the key on a bristling key ring and unlocked the door and swung it inward. Then he reached inside the door and flipped a light switch. He did not, however, sweep her up into his arms. "Welcome to Mockingbird," he said.

Amber didn't sigh or show disappointment in any way. Maybe the magic would take a little longer to happen. But he would feel what she felt, too. She knew it.

Amber entered the house and breathed in deeply. Every house has its own smell, she thought. Hers smelled of eucalyptus and vanilla candles, the fading pungence of the cleansers she liked and the coffee and cinnamon toast she had for breakfast nearly ever day.

And this house, she thought, this house also has its own scents: wood, leather and furniture polish. Somewhere inside was a library filled with old books, and there must be hardwood floors—polished recently with paste wax. Flowing inside through the open door came the incomparable sweetness of cedar and newly baled hay drying somewhere close by.

Amber's sandals tapped quietly on the floor. The entryway was part of the old construction, and centered under a hammered tin light fixture, a scarred round table rested on native flagstones. To the right she saw a dining room and hanging over the wall-size fireplace, a portrait photograph of a handsome, fair-haired man and his equally handsome son.

Bradley closed the front door, dropped his keys on the table and came and stood beside her. "Pope," he said, "and my dad when he was eleven."

"You look exactly like your grandfather," Amber said.

"Everyone says so."

Amber thought it odd that Bradley didn't sound happy when he said that. She knew—everyone knew—that Bradley had adored Pope. She assumed the comparison would flatter him.

She wondered about it as he led her through the rest of the downstairs. The new parts of the house had been designed to complement the environment—all native stone and cured hardwoods. The kitchen was a gourmet's dream, enormous and open. State-of-the-art enameled fixtures and appliances blended beautifully with Spanish tile, and the deep, wide windows would make this a bright, cheerful heart to the house.

On the other side of the entryway, an enormous family room walled in glass looked out over rugged, uneven ground that sloped down to a stream. One long wall was dominated by an antique bar that must have come from a mining saloon, and a polished concert grand piano sat gleaming and silent—just begging, Amber thought, for sensitive, nimble fingers. Through the glass wall opposite the bar, Amber saw the pristine white boards of a corral. Dark figures moved in the moonlight. Horses.

Although it was too dark to see the little arm of the Blanco River, when Bradley took Amber out onto the enormous deck, she could hear the endless, soothing murmur of water over rocks.

"When I was growing up," he said, "my cousins and I would all sit out here and have contests—boys against girls—to count the most falling stars."

"We do that at the beach," Amber said. "Our beach house is my favorite place. Like this is for you, I guess."

They stood close together, breathing in the sweet night air and enjoying the quiet moment. Amber realized they had come to an unspoken decision not to discuss their troubles just yet. Tomorrow would be soon enough for that, but for now they had stepped out of that life into this island of peace and serenity.

A thin brilliant line flashed overhead in the southern sky. "Look," Amber said. "That's one for the girls."

Bradley chuckled. "Why don't I get us a drink, and we can start this competition officially."

In a few moments he reappeared with glasses, a cool bottle of Chardonnay and a enormous quilt which he threw over the hard slats of the wooden glider swing. The chains creaked pleasantly, and the wine was sweet and cool. Bradley moved them back and forth with his foot, and Amber sat staring up into the calm night sky. "This is probably the most beautiful place I've ever seen."

"I think so, too. I can't believe anyone would want to destroy it."

The question hung in the air for a moment, and then Amber asked it. "Why does he want to, Bradley? If your dad hates the ranch and the company so much, why does he want to keep them? And what would he live on if he destroyed Ackerman?"

"My mother's trust money," he replied tersely. "You see, my dad sees the ranch and the company as extensions of his father. He hated Pope, and obliterating everything Pope spent his life building would be sweet revenge."

"Revenge for what?"

For a long moment Bradley was still, and though he gazed out at the winking stars and into the dark, soft sky, Amber knew his thoughts had gone elsewhere—he was staring across time into a distant and painful past. "My dad and Pope never got along, they were just too different. Grandy told me that when dad was young, he was interested in music and art. He liked the theater, too. He wanted to be an actor."

Bradley took a drink of wine. "That horrified my grandfather. He was an oil man, born and bred in Lubbock, Texas, in the twenties. Anyone who liked that fine arts stuff just wasn't a very manly man to Pope's way of thinking, so he did everything he could do to make my dad over in his own image. Any time Dad showed interest in something that wasn't masculine enough for my grandfather, well—Pope spoiled it for him or ridiculed him. He didn't mind if other people were around, either."

"Your poor dad."

"Yeah, well... I'm sure Pope loved him. They just couldn't understand each other. Pope raised my dad the way he thought best, and that included military schools, summer jobs on the rigs—that kind of thing." He leaned over, picked up the bottle and poured more wine into his glass and Amber's. "My father hated it all. Pope eventually got his way. My dad gave up his own dreams and tried to be what Pope wanted, but it poisoned their relationship."

Bradley shook his head. "No one ever heard one kind or encouraging word pass between Pope and my dad. They never hugged, never touched. And later on Dad met my mother, and she got pregnant." He smiled without joy.

"Pregnant with me. Pope forced my dad to marry her. And to stay married. He would have cut Dad off without a cent if he hadn't."

Even in the dim starlight Amber saw Bradley's jaw working. "My mother adores him still. I don't know why, either. The way he's treated her . . . is unforgivable." His voice fell to a mutter. "One more female casualty of the Ackermans."

"So I've heard," she murmured sympathetically.

Bradley turned to her, his confusion evident. "What?"

"I mean, I've heard gossip that your dad . . . your father isn't faithful."

"You're kidding. My father unfaithful?" Bradley laughed. "Phillip Ackerman isn't interested in other women. The truth is, I think he might even love my mother in his own way, he's just so full of bitterness now that that's all he has to offer. No, he doesn't look at other women, all he lives for is to be a big shot with his cronies and to destroy everything that reminds him of his father. I can guarantee you he's never strayed."

"But you said another casualty of the Ackermans."

"My dad never had other women, Amber. Pope did. He was unfaithful to Grandy for years. He loved her, he just couldn't—or wouldn't—be true to her. I think he may have been early on, but things changed. He did the best he could, he just didn't love her the way she loved him. It didn't break her spirit, but it broke her heart."

Amber sat quietly. Everything fell into place. That's why Bradley wouldn't accept the love and affection she offered. He thought he was protecting her. Since he looked exactly like his grandfather on the outside, he must have assumed he was like him on the inside, too.

"Look." Bradley pointed suddenly at another trail of light blazing across the sky. Wine splashed out of his glass and onto Amber's arm. "Damn," he said. "Did I get that on you?"

"I'm okay. Is the quilt all right?"

"It's nothing. It's old."

She brushed at the cool liquid, and Bradley set his glass down on the deck. He took her arm and swept his fingers from the inside of her elbow down to her wrist. He paused, then did the same thing again, more slowly. The touch turned into a caress, a slow trail of fingers awakening nerve endings.

Amber tilted her face up, and over the eaves of the house the benign face of the moon looked down, silvering the air and dusting everything around her in pale light. Amber's arms were naked, and her hair fell around her face, still tousled, she knew, from their windy ride. She felt him looking at her mouth and knew he desired her. She reached up and touched his face.

He leaned closer, and she moved toward him and rested her hand on his thigh. She heard him sigh and knew an inner resolve was crumbling. At first their mouths touched gently—a tentative exploration. A slow tasting to be savored. She touched his lips with her tongue, inviting a deeper intimacy.

"Amber," he groaned, and tangled his hands through her hair and trailed kisses down her throat to the hollow where her pulse throbbed. She curved her head down and kissed his neck. She let her teeth and tongue graze the sensitive skin just beneath his ear. He moaned aloud.

All at once he gathered her to him, and she wrapped her arms around his neck. Her love. Her husband. She knew the moment might pass and be gone forever, so she seduced him unashamedly with her mouth and her hands. She touched him every way that instinct told her, and beneath her hands his flesh ignited. She tugged his shirt from his pants and felt his smooth, warm skin, even as his fingers opened the buttons of her shirt.

She draped one leg over his and curved against the muscles of his thigh. He groaned, caught Amber's hand in his and pressed it down between his legs. Yes, he desired her. One of his hands slipped behind her, unhooked her brassiere and freed her breasts. She curved her head back, and he leaned down and took one rosy nipple into his mouth.

With a growl of frustration he stood and pulled her up, then swept the quilt onto the deck and laid her down on it. He undressed her in the moonlight, kissing, nuzzling and devouring every inch of her flesh. When he pulled his shirt off and threw it aside, Amber's breath caught. He was sculpted as perfectly as a statue, ridged and furrowed with hard muscle.

Within moments he knelt naked, poised over her in a fleeting second of hesitation. "Amber," he said, his voice hoarse with passion, "I don't want to hurt you. I—"

She sat up and silenced him with her mouth and hands, and when he entered her they joined in perfect accord in an ancient rhythm. He brought her with him to a quivering peak of satisfaction and then plunged over the edge with her, moaning her name into her mouth. And as he took her into that sweet abyss she spoke to him.

"I love you, Bradley."

Hours later he slipped from the bed where earlier he'd carried her and made love to her again. And again. She'd fallen asleep curled in his arms, replete and content. She'd asked him to leave the curtains open, and the moon was now high, old and small against the expanse of dark sky.

The pale light fell on her face, the sweet curve of her mouth and the soft tangle of her silky hair. Her bare shoulder was smoothly perfect, and he could just make out the swell of her breasts now dusky and chafed in the aftermath of his hungry kisses.

He looked down at her and once more felt the stirring of desire. He dragged his hand across his face. The movement was reflected back at him in the mirrored doors of the armoire across the room. Bradley faced his reflection.

"You bastard," he muttered. Quietly he opened a dresser drawer, pulled out pajama bottoms and tightened them with a savage yank of the waist cord. Then he walked through the silent house to the bar, poured himself two fingers of his father's Scotch and waited for the night to pass.

As the night grew old, he berated himself. You just couldn't leave her alone, could you? You couldn't keep your hands off her, not for one lousy day. She's done nothing but be kind and sweet and wonderful to you and your family, and look how you've paid her back. This fake marriage is going to humiliate her in front of everyone you know and probably damage her relationship with her family, too. And not only that, you've cost her the job she needs to finish her education. You know she's too proud to take money from you.

But that's not all is it? *I love you, Bradley.*

So Spencer had been right. *Now for your crowning achievement, you'll break her heart.*

He'd known all along to stay away from her. Every instinct told him so. Every time he was around her, hell, even from the first time he'd seen her, something told him to stay away. After each time they were together, he felt awful, suffered aching regrets or horrible feelings of guilt. He should have confined himself to the kind of women he'd always gone out with—wise, sophisticated, a little tough but unburdened by illusions.

I love you, Bradley.

Well, maybe he'd been weak before—even now he felt again an urgency gathering itself deep inside him. She'd been so sweet, so passionate. The things she said, the way she tasted, everything about her made his blood race. There was no question—if she stayed with him, he wouldn't be able to keep his hands off her. He would hurt her again and again; he couldn't stop himself.

He was, despite his fine intentions, just another man in the finest Ackerman tradition.

By the time she woke up, the morning sun was high, and the sight of her stumbling into the kitchen, sexy and small in the shirt he'd been wearing the day before almost doused his resolve. Then she looked up and smiled at him with eyes sweet and trusting. "Good morning," she said.

"We have to talk, Amber."

The minute Amber saw the look on his face, her heart filled with dread. *But I don't want to talk. Not yet.*

She knew he hadn't slept; he looked exhausted. But there was more. A part of her even knew what was coming though she denied it until the last minute. She wanted to cover her ears with her hands, to deafen herself to what he was saying, but she stood there—nearly naked, the cold stone floor biting her feet as he told her that she had to go. That he didn't love her. Could never love her.

"It isn't you, it's me, Amber."

Oh, yes. That's what they always say, isn't it?

"I'll tell Grandy what we did and why," he said. "But I want you to know I'll take care of your school tuition. And you know I'll be glad to support you in other ways, too. Please let me do this for you...."

She listened for as long as she could, but so much of what he said was drowned out by the buzzing, a sound like swarming hornets, that filled her head and blackened her vision until all she saw was his sad, intense face telling her over and over that he just didn't love her.

"Keep your money, Bradley," she said.

She forced her legs to move. She found her clothes neatly folded on a chair by the door. She'd left them outside last night, tangled with his like the silhouettes of lovers in the moonlight. She pulled the wedding ring off her hand and left it on the chair, unable to endure the sight of it another moment.

She heard him offering to drive her someplace—as if she could bear to be in a car with him. Then he offered her his car, but she couldn't drive the stick shift, so he gave her the keys to the Jeep. He would have loaded her bag for her, but she couldn't stand the thought of him watching her drive away alone.

Bradley pushed against the floor of the deck, and the swing moved with a sad creak. The Jeep had disappeared around a stand of junipers, and dust had long since settled. He'd been sitting there for a while, waiting for the ache in his middle to subside. The pain just got worse.

He'd hurt her. Bad.

"You deserve to feel guilty," he said. Every time he looked down and saw the place where they'd made love, the tightness in his chest got worse. He remembered her face, bright and flushed in passion. Her flat, warm stomach. And her lips and hands. God, she felt good. She made him feel good.

But there was more than that. She was sweet and smart and pretty. And so kind. She deserved better than him. She deserved someone who would love her the way she deserved—not someone who'd take everything she had to offer, then betray her. Even if he could remain faithful, he'd just never feel about her the way she felt about him—

he could never feel that way about any woman. For a long time he'd known exactly what he was.

And to his way of thinking, there was no bigger betrayal than love accepted but unrequited. Look what Pope had taken from Grandy; look what Phillip had done to his mother.

He couldn't do that and live with himself. No decent man could do that and feel good. A man had to feel good about himself—about his life.

As a matter of fact, now that he thought about it, Amber made him feel downright bad. Actually, she always had. Since he was searching his conscience, he had to admit she was the only woman who'd ever made him feel so miserable. He'd felt jealous and protective at their engagement party. No one he'd ever dated had made him feel that way before. She made his head hurt. And his stomach. And his heart.

He tried to make himself get up and do something. He sure as hell didn't want to sit there and wallow in his misery. He needed to talk to someone. But the only person he wanted to talk to was Amber. He missed her sweetness, her understanding. The way she made him feel like everything was going to be all right. The ache in his middle increased.

I suppose I should have seen it coming, he thought. How could I have been so blind? That thought stopped him. He'd always picked the women around him carefully. He'd always avoided hurtful, emotional entanglements. Well, maybe Tovah, but they'd been friends since they were kids. He wasn't in love with Tovah, but he loved her.

But I don't love Amber the same way, he thought. *Then how do you love Amber?*

He frowned. Well, he thought, he sure didn't want to hurt her. He wanted her to be happy, to get her degree and teach kids like she planned. He wanted her to be safe and have nice things. A home. Children. *And who would be their father?*

Even the passing notion of another man making love to her made Bradley's jaw tighten and his hands ball into fists. Why, if anybody even tried to lay a hand on his wife he'd...

"Oh, my God," he thought, as realization slowly dawned. He jumped and checked his watch. She'd been gone less than an hour. He could catch her. He yanked open the patio door and was running toward the bedroom when he heard the front door close.

His heart leaped. *It's her. She's come back.*

He forced himself not to run. After all, he didn't want to knock her down. He turned and walked briskly into the foyer. The smile dropped from his face.

"Hello, Bradley."

"What are you doing here, Dad?"

Phillip Ackerman raised his shoulders in the parody of a shrug. "You said to get my stuff off your property, or you'd throw it in the Blanco." His expression grew sly and knowing. "And I know you're a man of your word, aren't you, son? A living monument to veracity." He made a great show of looking around. "My mother tells me I have a new daughter-in-law. Where's the blushing bride?"

"That's none of your business, and I'd appreciate it if you left now. And leave your keys, too. I'll have your guns and your booze sent to the house."

Phillip didn't move. If anything, his expression became even more gloating. "Don't tell me the little woman already fled. What happened, son? Did you tell her the real reason you married her?" Cold satisfaction made his eyes glitter. "You always thought you were so much better than me, didn't you? Everyone else did, too. Grandy, the old man—everybody. Everybody said I was weak and no-good because I did what I had to do to keep my shares. Because I stayed married to your mother for the money. Everyone was so quick to point a finger and accuse me, but you're no different from me, are you? You did exactly the same thing. You married her to keep the property, didn't you? I knew you would. I just wanted everyone else—especially you—to see you're no different from me."

Bradley took a slow breath. "Dad, I couldn't begin to explain the ways I'm different from you. The first is maybe I'm willing to rear up on my hind legs and finally do something that scares me. Like admitting that I love my wife. That if I don't get to spend the rest of my life sleeping with her and laughing with her and fighting with her, my life might just turn out as miserable as yours."

Time was passing, and Bradley wanted to leave, but something else needed to be said. "The second is, I don't go sneaking around if I wanted to hurt a man—I do it right to his face. And though I love you, Dad, and I haven't hit another person since I was in junior high, if you're not out of my house in three minutes, I'm going to break your nose."

Chapter Eleven

Amber drove south for hours. She passed through the pretty little hill country towns down to the sloping monotony of Interstate 10 highway, leading back to Houston. She circled the city, an anthill of crawling traffic, and drove through the resort communities and over the causeway to Galveston. Then on through Galveston to Bolivar and onto the ferry. She watched the screaming, scavenging sea birds that dove into the churning water to snatch and devour the helpless life forced to the surface by the grinding propellers.

She knew her parents' beach house would be empty. They rarely came there during the week. She parked the Jeep, walked down to the water and sat in the dark, wet sand. Foamy breakers rolled in and receded, over and over, relentless and incessant.

To Amber it seemed she was seeing herself from a distance. Some pain, she realized, was too much to endure.

An inner defense mechanism engages and terminates all feeling before the pain becomes lethal.

She had heard that you could die of a broken heart.

An objective calm settled over her. This, she thought, is how her mother felt when they told her that Daddo was so sick. Maude lives with this every day. And this is how Violet felt when her father rejected her. And this is how Blanche Ackerman feels all the time. And Grandy, and so many others.

Amber remembered what Scarlet had said the last time they were together at the beach house. She'd called Amber's old boyfriends "Amber's Legion of the Lovelorn." Had she really made others feel what she was feeling now? This eviscerating emptiness?

Could this be the inevitability she'd sensed the moment she saw Bradley Ackerman? Is this, she wondered, what love is really about?

Eventually she went inside. She showered, but didn't eat. The rest of that day passed in a daze, as did the next. And the next.

Thursday she again sat at the tide line and watched the crabs and shore birds. She'd missed more school. It hardly mattered. She'd have to withdraw, anyway. She was going to have to go to work during the day. Maybe she'd take a class or two in the fall semester, if any of the classes she needed were offered at night.

How long would it be now, she wondered, until she finished. It didn't even matter.

Amber watched the families and beachcombers and shell seekers wandering up and down the water's edge. Sometimes they spoke to her, and sometimes she spoke back. Eventually she became aware that someone had come up behind her and halted only a few feet away, staring at her with a gaze that caused the flesh on her nape to prickle.

He came and sat down beside her, but didn't try to touch her. "I've been looking for you," Bradley said. "You scared me."

"How did you find me?"

"Your personnel file. Your sisters' numbers are there in case of emergency."

"What do you want?"

She saw the uncertainty in his face. And fear, too. She'd never seen him unsure of himself.

"I want you to come home, Amber." He held out the worn, gold wedding ring. "I want you to take this back and wear it. For real, I mean."

"Why?"

"Because I love you. I think I've loved you since the minute I saw you in the parking garage. You probably don't remember, but—"

"I remember."

"Well, ever since then you've never left my mind. I've never loved anybody before. Hell, I didn't know what I was feeling. I even thought I was coming down with something. You see, every time I was around you, I wound up feeling sick. At first I figured it was just guilt, and then I realized I never felt bad when you were around. Only when you left."

He reached out to her, and she let him take her hand and hold it. She thought she felt his warm pulse beating against her cold palm.

"And when you left the ranch, within thirty minutes I was going insane. I wanted to come after you—"

"Why didn't you, then?"

"Well, someone came by, and then the damn car wouldn't start."

Amber had to laugh. "Oh, Bradley. Get rid of it."

"I will. Anyway, I had to call one of the neighbors to come and get me and drive me to Austin. I flew back to Houston, but you weren't home. I called your sister, and she hadn't seen you, and your parents didn't know where—"

Amber felt a surge of protective outrage. "You didn't tell them, did you?"

"No, I just said I was your boss, and we wanted you to come in and work."

"How did you find me?"

"Your father's—Daddo's—name is in your personnel file. I knew there was beach property in his name. I just did a search in the deed records."

"Oh."

"So will you, Amber? Will you come back?"

She looked at his face, handsome, hopeful—so sure of himself and of her love. "No, Bradley," she replied. "I won't."

She saw the words cut into him. "You're angry with me."

"No. To tell you the truth, right now I don't feel much of anything. But I do know this. I love you. More than I ever imagined. More than I thought possible. For the first time in my life I really love someone, and I can't stand it. I want it to go away. It hurts too much."

"Amber," he said slowly. "This is my fault for being so stupid. I didn't think I could love anyone, and I thought that even if I did, I'd be like Pope and wind up changing my mind and breaking her heart." His hand closed a little tighter around hers. "I'll never forgive myself for hurting you the way I did. And I know I can't take it back, but I also know that real love doesn't go away. And I really love you, Amber. And I know you really love me, too—there's nothing you can do about it. It won't go away. So you might as well resign yourself to the fact that you're stuck with me, or at least with loving me, for the rest of your life. Don't you think it would be more convenient if we did it in the same house? Together? After all, we're married." He held the ring out to her again. "Remember?"

The numbness around her heart began to dissipate, like fog burned away by the rising sun. She smiled in spite of herself. "Maybe you should give that back to Grandy and get me one of my own."

Bradley's expression became unreadable. "I can't give it back to her."

Amber felt another clutch of fear. "She's not—"

"Oh, no, no. Nothing like that. It's just that she's got a new one."

"A new what?"

"A new wedding ring. She and Spencer eloped on Monday, right after we left."

"What?"

"Yes. It seems they've been planning this for years. Spence loved Grandy all his life, but she was devoted to Pope. After he died, she said she wasn't going to change anything until she was sure the company was taken care of. And that her family would be all right. She wanted to make sure that I was going to be chairman."

"Am I understanding you? Did the two of them orchestrate any of this?"

"Amber," he said, slowly, "we would have found each other eventually. I know now that we were meant to be together. But I'm afraid the fact remains that the two of us were completely outfoxed by a couple of old people."

She grinned. "You're kidding."

"No. I'm serious."

"But her health—"

"—is fine. The spells were caused by the pills she was taking. Her doctor—her former doctor—had given her the wrong prescription. Whenever she took them, she had that horrible reaction, but as soon as they wore off, she was fine. I think it's just possible, though, that she wasn't quite as sick as she seemed to be the day we got married."

"Then she's—"

"Healthy as a horse and on her way to Egypt with her husband. We think. Spence explained everything in the note he left me, resigning from the company. He said he'd been waiting for Grandy for fifty years. He figured that was long enough. She resigned, too. Actually, it would be good if you could get your adorable rear end moving. You've got a history paper due, and I've got a company to run. With Grandy gone, I'm the only Ackerman left on the board of my grandfather's company."

"But what about your dad?"

"The board fired him, and Blanche kicked him out of the house. Suzette went into labor, and Blanche decided she'd had enough of his . . . enough of him."

"Permanently?"

He shrugged. "Who knows. You know how true love is. Maybe she'll just scare the heck out of him and take him back once he's learned his lesson."

Amber laughed and kissed her husband on his mouth. He took her left hand and slipped her wedding band onto her finger. "Your engagement ring is being sized," he said.

"I'd love you no matter what, but I don't want you to have to gain fifty pounds just to keep from losing it."

She kissed him again.

"I've got an idea," he said.

"What?"

"Let's get married."

"But we already are married, Bradley."

"No, I mean a big one—all the bells and whistles. When Grandy and Spence get back."

"Do you want to?"

"I think we should."

"But the marriage we have already is the real one."

"Yes," he said. "It would just be a make-believe marriage."

"I like that kind."

"Me, too. Sometimes they lead to the most wonderful things."

* * * * *

Wedding Announcement

Amber Louise Oakland became Mrs. Bradley Alan Ackerman today in a double-ring ceremony at the Holy Word Chapel. Ms. Zita Bloom of Houston served as maid of honor, and the bride was also attended by her sisters, Miss Violet Fortescue and Miss Scarlet O'Reilly, both of Galveston, and the groom's sister, Miss Adelle Ackerman of Carmel, California.

After the ceremony the groom's grandmother, Mrs. Estelle Bailey, and her husband feted the couple and three hundred fifty guests at Columbine Hall.

The bride is a student in the School of Education at the University of Houston. The groom is president and chairman of the board of Ackerman Drilling Company.

The couple will split their time between their residences in Houston and Mockingbird Ranch in the Texas hill country.

Minneapolis, Minnesota

As Caroline Fortune wheeled her dark blue Volvo into the underground parking lot of the towering, glass-and-steel structure that housed the global headquarters of Fortune Cosmetics, she glanced anxiously at her gold Piaget wristwatch. An accident on the snowy freeway had caused rush-hour traffic to be a nightmare this morning. As a result, she was running late for her 9:00 a.m. meeting—and if there was one thing her grandmother, Kate Winfield Fortune, simply couldn't abide, it was slack, unprofessional behavior on the job. And lateness was the sign of a sloppy, disorganized schedule.

Involuntarily, Caroline shuddered at the thought of her grandmother's infamous wrath being unleashed upon her. The stern rebuke would be precise, apropos, scathing and delivered with coolly raised, condemnatory eyebrows and in icy tones of haughty grandeur that had in the past reduced many an executive—even the male ones—at Fortune Cosmetics not only to obsequious apologies, but even to tears. Caroline had seen it happen on more than one occasion, although, much to her gratitude and relief, she herself was seldom a target of her grandmother's anger. And she wouldn't be this morning, either, not if she could help it. That would be a disastrous way to start out the new year.

Grabbing her Louis Vuitton tote bag and her black leather portfolio from the front passenger seat, Caroline stepped gracefully from the Volvo and slammed the door. The heels of her Maud Frizon pumps clicked briskly on the concrete floor as she hurried toward the bank of elevators that would take her up into the skyscraper owned by her family. As the elevator doors slid open, she rushed down the long, plushly carpeted corridors of one of the hushed upper floors toward the conference room.

By now Caroline had her portfolio open and was leafing through it as she hastened along, reviewing her notes she had prepared for her presentation. So she didn't see Dr. Nicolai Valkov until she literally ran right into him. Like her, he had his head bent over his own portfolio, not watching where he was going. As the two of them collided, both their portfolios and the papers inside went flying. At the unexpected impact, Caroline lost her balance, stumbled, and would have fallen had not Nick's strong, sure hands abruptly shot out, grabbing hold of her and pulling her to him to steady her. She gasped, startled and stricken, as she came up hard against his broad chest, lean hips and corded thighs, her face just inches from his own—as though they were lovers about to kiss.

Caroline had never been so close to Nick Valkov before, and, in that instant, she was acutely aware of him—not just as a fellow employee of Fortune Cosmetics but also as a man. Of how tall and ruggedly handsome he was, dressed in an elegant, pin-striped black suit cut in the European fashion, a crisp white shirt, a foulard tie and a pair of Cole Haan loafers. Of how dark his thick, glossy hair and his deep-set eyes framed by raven-wing brows were—so dark that they were almost black, despite the bright, fluorescent lights that blazed overhead. Of the whiteness of his straight teeth against his bronzed skin as a brazen, mocking grin slowly curved his wide, sensual mouth.

"Actually, I *was* hoping for a sweet roll this morning—but I daresay you would prove even tastier, Ms. Fortune," Nick drawled impertinently, his low, silky voice tinged with a faint accent born of the fact that Russian, not English, was his native language.

At his words, Caroline flushed painfully, embarrassed and annoyed. If there was one person she always attempted to avoid at Fortune Cosmetics, it was Nick Valkov. Following the breakup of the Soviet Union, he had emigrated to the United States, where her grandmother had hired him to direct the company's research and development department. Since that time, Nick had constantly demonstrated marked, traditional, Old World tendencies that had led Caroline to believe he not only had no use for equal rights but also would actually have been more than happy to turn back the clock several centuries where females were concerned. She thought his remark was typical of his attitude toward women: insolent, arrogant and domineering. Really, the man was simply insufferable!

Caroline couldn't imagine what had ever prompted her grandmother to hire him—and at a highly generous salary, too—except that Nick Valkov was considered one of the foremost chemists anywhere on the planet. Deep down inside Caroline knew that no matter how he behaved, Fortune Cosmetics was extremely lucky to have him. Still, that didn't give him the right to manhandle and insult her!

"I assure you that you would find me more bitter than a cup of the strongest black coffee, Dr. Valkov," she insisted, attempting without success to free her trembling body from his steely grip, while he continued to hold her so near that she could feel his heart beating steadily in his chest—and knew he must be equally able to feel the erratic hammering of her own.

"Oh, I'm willing to wager there's more sugar and cream to you than you let on, Ms. Fortune." To her utter mortification and outrage, she felt one of Nick's hands slide insidiously up her back and nape to her luxuriant mass of sable hair, done up in a stylish French twist.

"You know so much about fashion," he murmured, eyeing her assessingly, pointedly ignoring her indignation and efforts to escape from him. "So why do you always wear your hair like this...so tightly wrapped and severe? I've never seen it down. Still, that's the way it needs to be worn, you know...soft, loose, tangled about your face. As it is, your hair fairly cries out for a man to take the pins from it, so he can see how long it is. Does it fall past your shoulders?" He quirked one eyebrow inquisitively, a mocking half smile still twisting his lips, letting her know he was enjoying her obvious discomfiture. "You aren't going to tell me, are you? What a pity. Because my guess is that it does—and I'd like to know if I'm right. And these glasses." He indicated the large, square, tortoiseshell frames perched on her slender, classic nose. "I think you use them to hide behind more than you do to see. I'll bet you don't actually even need them at all."

Caroline felt the blush that had yet to leave her cheeks deepen, its heat seeming to spread throughout her entire quivering body. Damn the man! Why must he be so infuriatingly perceptive?

Because everything that Nick suspected was true.

* * * * *

To read more, don't miss
HIRED HUSBAND
by Rebecca Brandewyne,
Book One in the new
FORTUNE'S CHILDREN *series,*
beginning this month and available only from
Silhouette Books!

MILLION DOLLAR SWEEPSTAKES